SIR

D.L. HESS

THE AWAKENING SERIES
BOOK ONE

DLHess.com

Join the mailing list and become a **D.L. Hess Insider**!
You can also **<u>Go Behind the Curtains</u>** to read about the making of *Sir* and get the inside scoop on the exciting adventures the author has in store for *The Awakening Series* at
<u>DLHess.com/blog/</u>!

You can also follow the author on
Twitter, Instagram, and Facebook.
<u>@DLHessWrites</u>

Cover design by Dharti Trivedi
Illustration by Samantha Hess and designed by Elijah Oliver

Text copyright © 2017 Dorian Hess/D.L. Hess
All Rights Reserved
ISBN: 9781549600388

For those who love and support me.
Especially my beloved B.

THE BEGINNING

I am a floating leaf
on the river of life
bobbing and bumping
along the bank

I yearn for you to guide me

expand my horizons
show me your world

enlightenment
pleasure
pain

I need you
I will be yours

Sir.

ONE

Tori

I wonder if I don't get out of bed, what will happen?

The obnoxious BWAMP-BWAMP-BWAMMP of my alarm and the flashing lights on my clock are telling me that I need to get moving if I don't want to be late to work.

It's not enough to motivate me to get out of bed.

I feel like I'm staring into the vast morass of my future and all I have to look forward to is the same monotony—work, sleep. Work, sleep. Work, sleep.

Nothing's changing. Nothing is going to change.

How did I get here? I ask myself for the thousandth time. *How did my life veer this far off course?*

I know the answer, of course. I know the decisions that led up to me living in Boden, Louisiana and working as a waitress at the local diner rather than being a doctor or a lawyer or whatever I

1

was meant to be. I know how stupid I was to make them. I know why I made them.

Love.

And a boy.

And if I'm not careful, I'm going to find myself married with three kids to the same boy-turned-man.

The horror of that thought is at least enough to get me to sit up and turn the blaring alarm off.

God, I really need something to change, I think as I roll out of bed to get started on my daily morning routine.

As I wash my hair under the lukewarm, low pressure shower stream—I should get that fixed—my thoughts go back to the boy-turned-man who I wrecked my life for.

Brady Boden.

Handsome Brady Boden, star LSU quarterback, son of one of the richest families in south Louisiana, lover of fast cars and even faster women.

And, somehow, he wanted me.

There I was, a naïve freshman, two months into college, from a small town in rural Iowa, on full scholarship at a major SEC university, and, for some unexplainable reason that I still don't understand, the most popular guy in the city asked me out.

I still wonder about that, even now, four years later, as I blow dry my hair. Out of the thousands of girls he could have chosen at LSU, why me?

I'll probably never get an answer, I think as I swipe on some mascara and Burt's Bees tinted lip balm before choosing my outfit-for-the-day, a soft green sweater and my favorite leggings. As I get dressed and meander to the kitchen to throw together a breakfast of cold leftovers and hot coffee, I think back on the rest of the story and how it led to me here, today.

I remember how Brady tried to move faster than I was comfortable with, and I let him because that's what I thought I was supposed to do, painfully losing my V-card on the second date in the back of his black Cadillac Escalade bought and paid for by the booster club.

He kept coming back, probably because he knew I was an easy lay and star-struck enough to hang on to every word he said like it was gold. He had a captive audience in me and he was handsome and charming enough that I completely deluded myself into believing that this was love.

We dated all semester and I pushed aside any rumors that he was sleeping with other girls. It didn't matter that he never took me as his date to team parties or made grand declarations that we were together. I bought his excuse that he had an image to uphold and that I wouldn't like the attention that dating him would shine on me.

I was an idiot.

The LSU Fighting Tigers made it to the National playoffs that year. Brady had an off game and ended up missing more passes than he connected. The night the team got back to campus, he drunk drove his Escalade into a tree. With one terrible decision, he shattered his knee and his chance to be drafted in the NFL.

He took a semester off to go back home to recuperate. He asked me to come with him over Christmas break to help, and like the love-dumb fool that I was, I followed him to a tiny town in the swamps outside of New Orleans that was named after his great-grandfather. The same man who built the petroleum processing facility that now employees nearly everyone who lives in the shadows of its smokestacks.

I was too distracted to realize that I had a delinquent fee bill that I needed to pay to stay enrolled and start classes. (Months later, I discovered that the reminder email had somehow made it into my Trash folder.)

The thirty-dollar fee bill never got paid. I lost my scholarship and my housing and living stipends, but I brushed that all aside because Brady was also taking a semester off and he needed me. And isn't love all about sacrificing for the other person?

Like I said, idiot.

Particularly since we didn't live in happy love-fueled bliss where I played nursemaid to my war-battered hero. Brady is from a strict Catholic family.

"I won't allow you to live in sin with your harlot of a girlfriend. Not under my roof," his mother said as his dad leered at me over his glass of bourbon.

I no longer had my place at LSU and there was no place for me here... except during the day, when I was still expected to cater to Brady's every need. Apparently, harlots still make good nursemaids. Who'd have thought?

So around the same time classes were about to start without me, there I was, stuck in Boden, eighteen years old, homeless, jobless, with seven dollars left in my bank account from the previous semester's stipend. I had spent the last of my money on a sketchy roadside inn and I didn't know what to do or where to go.

Enter my guardian angel and soon-to-be best friend, Elizabeth St. Claire, owner and operator of the Finewhile Diner.

My well-worn black Converses scuff against the linoleum floor in Elizabeth's—and my—kitchen as I decide against the leftovers and drop some bread into the toaster and pull out a jar of homemade strawberry preserves from the refrigerator. As I stare at my mirrored reflection in the shiny toaster while waiting for my toast to pop up, I remember how Elizabeth saved me in my darkest hour.

I owe her everything.

Elizabeth inherited the diner from her parents when they decided to retire early and drive their motorhome to Boca Raton. She wasn't really looking for help, or a roommate, when she saw a helpless college dropout crying in the back booth of her restaurant at midnight.

Earlier that evening, I'd admitted defeat and called my mom for help. At first, it was like she didn't know who I was, screaming and cursing at me before hanging up. It was shocking and completely out of character for my loving and supportive single mother, but, in the moment, I felt like I deserved her rage. I threw my life and my future away for absolutely no reason. I hated myself. Why wouldn't she hate me too?

So I was sitting in the back of the diner with nowhere to go. I had been kicked out of the motel that morning, I was too afraid of my mom's disappointment and anger to call home again, and I was down to my last seven dollars—enough for a cup of coffee and a slice of pecan pie.

Elizabeth refilled my coffee, sat down across from me, and asked, "How can I help?"

I stared at her, gaping like a fish, blushing up a storm, unsure of how to respond.

"Honey," she said, reaching across the table to softly touch my hand, "I know what helplessness and self-loathing look like. I've been there too."

I told her every embarrassing detail that got me to that point—Brady, moving here only to have nowhere to stay, being Brady's nurse, getting kicked out of school, my mom's shocking anger…

Since I was the only customer in the diner, Elizabeth grabbed herself a slice of pie and a cup of coffee and sat back down with me.

"We're going to try to find a solution to your problem," she said, taking a bite.

I remember watching her chew, half wondering if she noticed the same thing about the pie that I did. I could tell by the taste and texture of the crust that the pie was bought pre-made in bulk and frozen. All pie is good, but there's nothing better than fresh, made-that-day pie so I was kind of picking on my piece. It took my mind off of the epic failure that my life had become.

"If you could be anything in the world, do anything, what would it be?" she asked between bites.

"I figured I'd become a doctor. Maybe a lawyer," I shrugged, looking away from her piercing gaze to watch my fork scrape through the crumbs on my plate. "It was still early. I had time to decide."

"And would being a super fancy, big time doctor/lawyer make all your dreams come true?" she asked, probably already knowing the answer.

"It'd make my mom happy." I shrugged again.

"If you don't mind me commenting on your life, it seems like you do too much to make others happy and not enough to make yourself happy," she stated, leaning back and sipping her coffee, her pie barely touched. "What's wrong with the pie? Don't like it?"

"It's not that," I hedged, not wanting to offend her, not sure why she changed the subject.

"Really? Because you just told me that you're spending the last of your money on that piece of pie and you're not eating it," she responded.

I jerked my head up to look at her, afraid that I made her angry. But by the way she was looking at me, she was more amused than angry.

"Pat, my fry cook, is great, but he sure can't bake worth a damn," she grinned. I think I smiled back.

"It's the preservatives," I clamped my mouth shut, worried that I'd said too much as it was.

Her eyebrow lifted, and it was one of the most intimidating looks I'd ever been on the receiving end of. "Go on. Tell me what's wrong with the pie."

So I told her about my suspicion that it was premade in bulk before being frozen and defrosted. How you could taste the preservatives and that hint of frozen freezer taste that made the pecans start to edge towards being rancid.

"I'm taking from this that you bake," she said, amusement in her voice.

I shrugged, not sure why she was asking. "Just as a stress relief."

"Just pie?"

"Cakes, pies, cookies, muffins… whatever sounds good," I replied.

"Are they any good?" she asked, the hint of a smile on the edges of her mouth.

"They're better than *this*," I said, pushing the mangled pecan pie away from her.

Her eyebrow went up again and it was hard for me not to sink underneath the table. I probably shouldn't have insulted her food.

"Ever waited tables before?"

"No, ma'am," I mumbled, embarrassed that I had just insulted my new confidante.

"Tori," she scoffed, "I'm, maybe, four years older than you. Don't call me ma'am."

I nodded. Probably shrugged. I shrugged a lot that night.

I remember that I started feeling really hopeless right about then, my thoughts becoming darker and darker. I did not know what I was going to do once I stood up from that table. I was afraid of what I *would* do.

"Here's what I'm thinking," Elizabeth said, breaking me out of my despair.

I remember glancing up at her and thinking she was really pretty, the kind of pretty that radiates from inside and shines through her sparkling blue eyes and the small smile she was giving me. I remember smiling back, even though I had so little hope left.

"You're going to work for me, here, at the diner. It pays half minimum wage, but you get to keep your tips. You're going to save that money and go back to college as soon as possible," she stated, as if it was a done deal.

"I can't—" I stuttered, shocked by her proposal, mind going a million miles an hour, finally landing on "I don't have anywhere to live."

"I'm not done," she said, that eyebrow going back up and pinning me to my seat. "Do you do drugs?" I shook my head no. "Drink?" No. "Smoke?" No. "Play loud music at 2 a.m.? Throw raging keggers on the weekends?"

I kept shaking my head, completely confused as to why she was asking these questions. It had been a long day and my brain was having problems catching up.

"Do you have a habit of sneaking strange men into your bedroom at night?" Elizabeth questioned with a straight face.

I laughed at that. "Before Brady I was a—"

She held her hand up to stop me. "*Really* don't need to hear the details."

I had to wonder, "Why are you asking all this?"

"Did I look like I was done interrogating you?" she asked sternly, blue eyes sparkling with merriment.

"No, ma'am," I replied. I was so confused that night, sitting in that booth with a woman—a girl, really—not much older than I was, who was offering me a lifeline.

"We'll need to work on that 'ma'am' thing," she said, shaking her head in mock annoyance. "Are you neat enough? Clean up after yourself? Cook occasionally?"

I nodded my head, realization slowly coming to me, shocking me that...

"If you're OK with kids—I have son but he's a good egg—I have an extra room in my house," Elizabeth stated. "It'll be tight and I may need you to help out some. If it turns out that it's not working out, you'll have to find a new place, but if it works out, I can rent it to you until you have your legs under you again."

"But I have no money," I couldn't help but say. Again.

"Pies, girl, keep up," Elizabeth scoffed, rolling her eyes, "You're paying me in baked goods."

My jaw dropped. "Wait. What?"

"You think I don't know I have crap pie? It's the worst thing on the menu. So you'll make yummy baked goods for me to sell and I'll let you use my spare room."

"You can't do that," I said, bowled over by her insane generosity. Towards me. A stranger. "People don't do things like that for other people."

"Really?" She grinned. "'Cause I think I just did."

~~~~~~

I walk down Magnolia Street to the diner, passing the strange, quaint little town that's taken me in and turned into home. The houses are small and some could handle some new paint or a fence repair, but the people inside of those houses tend to be honest, hard-working folks just trying to live their lives the best way they know how. They go to work, pay their bills, and take care of their families. That is their life. And, somehow, I've become one of them.

Elderly Mr. Johnson sits in a rocking chair on his postage stamp-sized front porch and raises his coffee cup to me as I pass, just like he does nearly every morning like clockwork. There's something about that gesture this morning that sends me back to thinking about that night in the diner five years ago, about how Elizabeth quite possibly saved my life with her offer of a room and a job.

I went home with her at the end of her shift, taking the same five-block, three-turn walk that I now take every day. I moved into her home that night and never moved out.

Months later, I asked her why she chose to help me. She looked up at the ceiling of her living room, in the direction of the

9

second upstairs bedroom where her son Benji lay sleeping, sighed, and said, "Because I know what it's like to meet a guy and have your whole life change in a moment because of him."

I think that was the moment that Elizabeth became my best friend as well as my boss and savior.

She helped me rebuild my life and save up money so that I could go back to school. She helped me keep my eye on the prize, while making sure I didn't overwork myself or give up. In a lot of ways, she became the big sister I never had.

She stood beside me when I was dumb enough to fall for Brady's BS again. Then she fed me ice cream and held me as I cried when I realized again how awful he really is.

When I got the phone call that my mother fell down some stairs and broke her hip, needing major surgery that she couldn't afford, Elizabeth helped me smash old dishes as I ranted and raved that I shouldn't have to help her since she didn't help me.

And she held my hair back from my face as I vomited into the toilet after the phone call I had with my mother's doctor when he told me that the reason my mother refused to help me was because she didn't know who I was. My mother had early onset Alzheimer's and would need to be put in a nursing home after her surgery. And I would be the one responsible for paying for her care.

The next paycheck, my salary had doubled. Though it wasn't much, Elizabeth gave me a raise because she knew that all that money I scrimped and saved was now going to go to a nursing home in Iowa and not to my college education.

That little raise stopped me from asking for a loan from Brady and indebting me to him for life.

Elizabeth really is my savior, I think for the thousandth time as I walk through the parking lot of the Finewhile Diner, the gravel crunching under my feet. I should talk to Elizabeth about getting it repaved. Business is the best it's ever been, and we've been working on slowly renovating it to its former glory.

And, I hate to brag, but it's become difficult keeping up with customers' demands for my cakes and pies.

I enter the diner, breathing in the smell of sizzling hamburgers and salty fries. Without knowing when it happened, the smell of the Finewhile Diner makes me feel safe, like I'm home.

I scan the customers, counting tables and orders. It's the end of the lunch rush and Elizabeth is the only one on the floor. I know everyone here except one guy in the back, whose head is hidden by the menu. His laptop is out, which probably means he's here for the free WiFi as much as he is for the food.

I nod to Elizabeth, indicating with my eyes that I'll be in back if she needs me. She nods and goes to her next table, refilling their coffee.

"Hey, Pat," I call out to the cook as I enter the kitchen.

"Hey there, pretty lady," he says back with a wink. Pat is African Creole, gorgeous, and the biggest flirt I've ever met. He's like that to everyone he meets, and his wife would probably string him up by his toes if she ever thought he was serious.

I throw on a full apron and get to work, making icing for the cakes I baked last night. My mind starts to drift back to Brady as I complete the familiar task.

If only I could learn how to shake him for good.

Like me, he never did go back to school. Instead, Daddy Dear, Braden Senior, took him under his wing and started teaching him how to run the refinery. Guess when it's the family business you don't need a college degree.

So Brady is always around, speeding through town in his too-big, overpriced Ford pickup truck, picking up whatever girl he can get. When he gets bored with the other women in town, he comes after me.

Sometimes I'm stupid enough to take him up on his offer. It's like I never learn my lesson. And I know if I'm not careful, I'm going to wake up one day with three kids, a dog, and a ring on my finger that labels me as Mrs. Brady Boden while he screws every other woman in the parish.

I have to shake myself out of my internal rant, returning my focus to slathering the last of the chocolate buttercream icing onto the vanilla cake in front of me. During the last sweep of my icing spatula, I hear Elizabeth call out, "Tori, I need you to take over, please," from the dining room.

As I walk through the swinging doors into the dining room, I come to the same conclusion I had earlier this morning:
I really need something in my life to change before it's too late.

TWO

Nate

I hate this fucking town.

I hate what it looks like. I hate the people in it. I hate what it represents (read: everything that's wrong with the United States).

I thought I had moved past my animosity in the years I've been away, but as my car thumps into another canyon-sized pothole, I decide that once I'm done with it, it can fucking fall off the map for all I care.

Hopefully when it does, it will take the filthy, smoke-filled single-wide trailer I grew up in and my bastard father, too.

God, I thought I was done with this place when I caught a one way Greyhound bus out of town twelve years ago. But, no, I realize as I slam on my breaks to avoid hitting a stray dog that darts in front of my car, this damn place sucks you back in whether you want to be here or not.

My gaze drifts up from the running dog to the massive oil refinery that towers over the entire town. Gray concrete pillars stab into the overcast sky, spewing out flame and steam to mix with the slow drizzle falling down onto the dreary streets below. It's a striking visual, one that's been imprinted on my brain since childhood.

Boden, Louisiana sits between the Mississippi River and the shores of Lake Pontchartrain, close enough to see the lights of New Orleans and yet a world away. The town built up around the Boden oil refinery in the 1920s, and its ugly soot gray smoke stacks loom over the town during the daytime. At night, between the bright work lights and flares from the gas burn off, you can see the refinery from forty miles away in any direction. The town is ugly, it's dirty, it's hopeless destitution sitting at the base of American capitalism.

It's the boil on the ass of Louisiana, and that's saying something.

And it's perfect for what I need to do.

It's surreal driving these familiar streets. There are a couple of new buildings here and there, all built cheaply for functionality not aesthetics, but for the most part, it's pretty much exactly how I remember—crumbling mom-and-pop stores, small houses with late model cars and trucks in the driveways, and stray kids and dogs darting out from between them. I left this damned town when I was eighteen, swearing to high heaven (and hell) that I'd never be back.

I guess I'm glad I didn't bet any money on it, because I would have lost the bet, I think with a rueful shake of my head as I turn past the entrance of the motor home park where I spent the first eighteen years of my life.

Growing up, the only plan my brothers and I had was to get out of Boden as soon as possible. Our father was a heavy drinker since before most of us were alive, and it only got worse as we got older. Our mom was amazing—kind, caring, beautiful,

14

smart. I know she was planning to save us from him, but she never had the chance.

Life got hard for awhile. My older brother Leo did what he could to deflect dad's rage, but Leo only had a few years left of high school before he escaped on a football scholarship to Harvard. Then it was just the younger three of us who did what we could to survive until we could get out too.

I was the next to leave, along with my youngest brother Felix, who's a genius and graduated at the same time I did. Unfortunately, my younger brother Chance had to wait a couple more years, but within three months of graduation, he was hopping a Greyhound to Seattle to play in a band.

My plan had always been to follow in Leo's footsteps and use football to get out of town, but a bad tackle led to a badly broken leg my junior year of high school and that route closed to me. The academics at the high school were a joke, but you actually have to show up to pass, so academic scholarships to college were out. By the time I realized the mess I was in, it was too late to fix my grades.

I was desperate to get out. I was tired of being poor, tired of living in a broken-down trailer on the rough side of town with a bitter man who drank too much, the memory of my dead mother, and brothers who were just as desperate as I was to escape. I wanted more from life than what Boden, Louisiana could give me. I didn't know what that was, but I knew it was out there ready for me to find it.

It wasn't until I saw an article in a used copy of a magazine left at the doctor's office about the best paid people in America that I figured out where I was going and how I was getting out…

My senior year, I auditioned for the school play after losing a bet. Not only did I land the lead role, but I also learned that I was a naturally gifted actor. Those precious moments performing on stage allowed me to push away my own problems and step into the shoes of someone else, someone who wasn't stuck in a dead in town with no future.

I realized that I didn't need to go to college to become a movie star. I just needed to move out to Los Angeles and chase my dream. I figured that it was there for the taking if I had enough balls to go for it. I knew that I had no problem with hard work, and even though my brother Chance got most of the attention, I could tell by the way girls—and occasionally their mothers—looked at me that I was attractive enough to be in movies. And no one has ever felt the need to question if I have balls.

I was sold.

I took the Greyhound out of town the night of my graduation and I was in L.A. two days later. It started out slow, of course. I auditioned for anything that would have me and was cast in a few student short films that went nowhere.

To pay the rent, I worked nights with a janitorial service that cleaned up a swanky Beverly Hills high rise that housed one of the biggest agencies in town. Six months into the pushing mops gig, I met a talent agent named Jim who was working late one night when I came in to empty his trash can. He liked my look, asked to see my audition reel, and recommended a few acting workshops.

A year later, Jim was representing me and I was getting real roles, first as an extra and in walk on parts, then, soon enough, I started landing speaking parts and supporting roles.

It wasn't until I finally landed a lead in a low budget independent film that my career really took off. One role led to another, then suddenly, one of those movies took off in the film festival circuit, and I started getting calls from the big studios around town.

I worked hard during the day, taking any job that looked half-way decent and wouldn't wreck my career if it flopped. At night, I was on the red carpet, in clubs, or at parties. And that's where the women were—wannabe actresses hoping that fucking a big name star would land them their break, starlets hoping to stay relevant and land an equally famous husband, and producers' wives looking for a distraction.

Flip through any celebrity gossip rag, point to a page, and there's a strong chance that I've slept with the woman on that page. I'm not going to say no to free and available pussy. I get it all, in every size, shape, color, and nasty proclivity. The kinkier, the better.

Nathanial Stone has been a very busy man.

And in between work and play, I took classes at UCLA. Because even though I had made it as an actor and I had more money than I knew what to do with—especially with Felix investing it for me—and even though women dropped their panties at the smallest glance, my ultimate goal was to be behind the camera. Growing up how I did, I have a thing for control, and the best way to be in control is to be a producer/director.

Now I finally have that chance. A studio is backing me on my first directorial role. I have a great script, a great cast, a great production team. All I needed was to find the location to shoot the film.

But after months of location scouting and years of hard work getting to this point, it became apparent that fate was laughing in my face and forcing me to come back to my childhood hometown.

Because the only place in the United States—the *world*— that was enough of a shit-stain for this film was goddamned Boden.

If it wasn't my big break into directing, I'd have scrapped the project already, turned around, and gone home.

I really hate this town.

I can't even get decent WiFi. I have to laugh about how pretentious and L.A. I sound, but I came back to Boden early to work on the minutiae of pre-production, which I can't do if I don't have reliable access to the internet.

I was promised that everything would be set up before I flew in this morning, but, instead, I arrived to discover that the cable company is dragging their feet to install the internet in the house I'm renting. Thus, I've been driving all over town looking for a coffee shop, Starbucks, *something* so that I don't lose more valuable time not being able to work. I finally had to pull over at a gas station to ask. The old man behind the counter didn't know what I was talking about, but the guy buying cigarettes behind me in line—who looked like he just got off work at the plant—said that there's only one place in town with a decent connection.

My tires crunch on gravel as I pull into the parking lot of one of the few places in Boden that hold good memories for me.

The Finewhile Diner.

Every Sunday afternoon while my mother was alive, she'd bring me and my brothers to the Finewhile for chocolate shakes and fries. It was here that she told us about her dream for us to see the world and get out of Boden. It was here that she told us that she was planning on leaving our father and taking us with her. Of course, she died before she ever got the chance.

But it was also at the Finewhile that I had my first kiss with Amanda Pinkerton when I was thirteen, our heads ducked below the cracked sea foam green vinyl booths. When I was fourteen, Mary Jane Bitford gave me my first blow job in the unlocked storage closet. A month later, I screwed her older sister Bethany out back in their daddy's car.

Good things happen at the Finewhile.

THREE

Nate

A surprisingly warm wave of nostalgia hits me as I step into the diner, the ringing bell over the door and the familiar scent of French fry grease in the air sends me straight back to high school.

The booths are now covered in bright cherry red vinyl that screams 1950s Americana. The chrome detailing shines like it's been recently polished and the vinyl seating isn't cracked and ragged like it was the whole time I was growing up. There's also art on the walls—vibrant oil paintings of 50s memorabilia that adds to the nostalgia. I have to assume the diner is under different management and that whatever else is happening in this struggling town, the Finewhile is doing well.

"Seat yourself!" yells the fry cook through the open window from the kitchen.

I end up in the back of the restaurant in a booth, away from the windows and next to a wall outlet. Since it's mid-afternoon most of the lunch crowd has gone back to work, leaving only a few old men sitting at the counter sipping at their coffees. The jukebox by the door that was added during my absence is playing Nat King Cole, and I decide that I can work with this.

I pull out my Macbook and easily find the Finewhile's network logon. The password is on a sign next to the register, so soon enough I'm buried in the pile of emails that has grown since this morning.

I hear the kitchen doors flap open and the call of "I'll be with you in a minute" from the waitress. I glance up to see a mane of bouncing gold ringlets pulled back into a pony tail atop a petite little thing in tight denim heading away from me.

I had resigned myself to having a dry spell for these few months while I was working, assuming that the women of Boden would be just as abysmal as the town they lived in. I figured that if I became desperate for a quick fuck, I could drive into New Orleans for a simple pickup at one of the French Quarter bars. However, maybe Boden has something to offer after all.

The waitress drops off her plates and heads over to me. I take advantage of her journey over here to get a good look at the front of her. She's barely over five feet tall, with those bouncing curls, bright blue eyes, and a mischievous tilt to her welcoming smile.

As if a line of checkboxes from my memory are checkmarked, I realize that I know exactly who she is. I have a vague memory from when I saw her last—a small girl hiding behind huge out-of-style eyeglasses and an oversized paint-splattered sweatshirt with hair that looked like she had stuck her finger in a light socket. But, really, I know this girl, this woman, walking towards me from hundreds of late night drunken phone calls from my brother Chance.

This is Chance's Lizzie, the girl he fell in love with the summer after high school. The girl he walked away from so he could become a rock star.

I can tell from the stutter in her step and the way her smile slips as the color leaves her face that she recognizes me too.

But I admire the way she straightens her shoulders and tilts her chin up. I can tell that it's hard for her to keep walking towards my table, that it's hard to keep the smile on her face. And even though I've met a thousand women arguably more beautiful, with that show of courage, I can tell exactly why my brother fell so hard.

"Welcome to the Finewhile Diner, my name is Elizabeth and I'll be taking care of you. Can I start you off with a cup of coffee? It's Community Coffee with chicory, is that alright?" she asks, bravely making eye contact even though I can tell she wants to be anywhere but here.

It seems like my brother did just as big a number on her as she did on him. I decide the only thing to do is address the Technicolor elephant in the room.

"I've heard a lot about you from my brother," I tell her, smiling softly to try to let her know that I'm no threat.

"I'm sure I don't know what you're talking about," she says, looking away, "If you're not going to order, I'm going to have to ask you to leave my restaurant."

"Coffee, please," I grin. I don't like that she's uncomfortable, but as a filmmaker, a studier of human emotions, I find this encounter fascinating.

She returns quickly, thumping the mug so hard on the table that the coffee sloshes over the side.

"I'm not going to tell him I've seen you if you don't want me to," I reassure her.

"I don't know who you're—" she stops mid-sentence, sighing in resignation as her shoulders fall down from around her ears. "You're one of Chance's brothers, aren't you?"

"Yes, I'm Nate," I reply, offering my hand to shake. She takes it. "You sure did leave an impact on my brother."

She glances out to the street, as if searching for something. "I can promise you, it was mutual."

"Chance told me that you were in Chicago."

"Things changed, I came back," she replies nonchalantly.

"Do you have a moment to sit?" I ask, not quite sure why I'm asking, but I assume it's to get to know the woman who's had my brother all tied up in knots for nearly a decade.

She glances around the diner, checking to see if anyone needs her before taking a seat on the creaking booth. "So you're Nathanial Stone, the big Hollywood actor. I remember waiting on you and all your friends back in high school. What brings you back to this rat trap?"

So she doesn't like Boden either. Interesting.

"I'm directing a movie in town for the next few months. I'm here early to work on pre-production before we get started on principle filming."

"I'd heard some big wig was shooting a movie here. I didn't realize it was one of the Stone boys," she exclaims, eyes sparkling with excitement. Yeah, I can definitely see what my brother saw in her.

But I can also tell when she catches herself and reins her emotions in.

"Have you seen your dad yet?" she asks.

I feel myself go cold at the question. I don't think there's anyone on the planet I loathe more than my father. I still blame him for my mother's death and the years of hell as he took his drunken anger out on my brothers and me. He's been dead to me since I stepped on that Greyhound and he can stay dead for all I care.

"I'll get there eventually," I lie.

"He's doing well," she replies. "I check in on him every few months, make sure he's doing OK." She pauses, waiting for me to say something, but I've got nothing good to say about that motherfucker. I'm somewhat surprised that she keeps up with him. If Chance ever told her even a quarter of what that man did to us, I would have thought that she'd hate him too.

"He's been sober for going on six years now," she continues, "He got back into woodworking last fall. He's pretty talented. But, then, talent, in general, seems to run in the family."

I sip at my coffee, momentarily regretting asking this pretty, talkative, brave young woman (who my brother's still hung up on) to sit.

"Do you ever talk to him?" she asks. "Is he doing OK?"

I can tell from the longing on her face that she's trying so hard to hide that she doesn't mean my father.

"It's Chance." I shrug. "You know how he is. Living life to the fullest."

"Yeah," she breathes out on a wistful sigh with a distant look in her eyes, probably thinking about the thousands of images out there of my brother singing to sell out crowds on stage or walking red carpets with gorgeous lingerie models on his arm.

I don't tell her that secretly Chance is miserable beneath his grinning façade, fucking anything that walks and drinking himself into an early grave.

One of the old geezers at the counter calls her over and she leaves me with a kind smile as she says with a wink, "Don't be a stranger, Nate. Feel free to camp out here and borrow my WiFi any time."

As I watch her walk away from me, a tickle of a thought about pursuing something with her while I'm in town flickers in the back of my mind. However, Chance's face the last time I saw him pops into my head. Even though he was slurring and could barely keep his eyes open, I believed him when he said he wishes that he never went to Seattle. That his greatest mistake was leaving the woman who was walking away from me.

Yeah, Elizabeth St. Claire is definitely off limits.

I turn back to my computer, mind still stuck on the mess my brother made with this woman when the woman in question suddenly yells out, "Tori, I need you to take over, please," as she runs out of the diner.

I crane to look out the window, trying to figure out the rush. Past the parking lot is a school bus letting off a bunch of kids. A couple of elementary school aged boys seem to be pushing another kid around. Some things just don't change.

The kitchen doors swing open, stealing my attention from Elizabeth running towards the schoolyard tussle. I glance over to see "Tori" step out of the kitchen.

I first notice her huge, guileless amber-green eyes above luscious pink lips—the kind of lips made for sucking cock. Mouthwatering breasts push against her soft green sweater. The sensual flare of her decadent hips beneath tight leggings. Her wavy chocolate-brown hair is trying to escape from the artless bun she has twisted on the top of her head, precariously held together with an ink pen, a picture of unaffected sensuality.

This woman is sexy as fuck, all ass and breasts and big green eyes, and I have a sneaking suspicion that she has no clue how she affects the men in the room.

As I watch her, she walks through the restaurant to check on each table, hundreds of obscene fantasies flash through my mind with her as the star, on and on, scene after scene: leather, handcuffs, gags, crops, floggers…

She'd be magnificent.

I may come to appreciate Boden after all.

FOUR

Tori

Holy mama llama.

That's Nathanial Stone. Nathanial Stone is sitting in my booth. Nathanial Stone is in the Finewhile Diner sitting in my booth.

I'm supposed to wait on Nathanial Stone.

I don't know how I recognized him across the restaurant. It's not like I watch many movies.

But I do see him often enough on the front pages of gossip magazines in the checkout lane at the grocery store. Since he first became famous, there was something about him that drew me in. I would secretly study his stunning face on the glossy cover as I'd wait in line, fingers itching to buy it just so I could look a little longer. He's always pictured with some gorgeous woman with a perfect body and a glamorous life. Usually the caption has something to do with how he's broken up with the actress/model/singer and the woman is devastated.

I'd be devastated too if someone like him broke up with me.

I'm not a fan, though, I don't think. Not in the strictest definition. I don't stalkishly follow his life. I don't seek out any small detail of his likes or habits besides what is general pop culture knowledge. I only knew he was from Boden because one of the first things you're told when you arrive in town is about the town's greatest success story, the Stone boys: the two billionaires (one's a bio-tech entrepreneur, the other's a wunderkind investment manager), the Grammy Award winning rock star, and the Hollywood movie star.

And the movie star Stone is right there, looking back at me.

Oh, crap. I'm supposed to be waiting on him right now.

I feel my cheeks flush and my palms go sweaty. I have a rush of adrenaline and I think this is what an out-of-body experience feels like.

I'm going to make a fool out of myself. I just know it. I can *feel* it coming.

Crap.

I look around, hoping I can postpone the indignity of stuttering like a lunatic in front of the sexiest man alive—according to *People* magazine, *twice*—while giving him crazy eyes.

Of course, everyone looks like they're taken care of. Except for Mr. Sexypants, major Hollywood actor, Nathanial Stone, Sir.

I glance out the front window, hoping Elizabeth is on her way back, but, nope, of course not. She's still dealing with the bullies at the bus stop.

I sigh. Looks like I'm going to have to suck it up and get over myself.

He's a person, just like any other customer, do your job, I try to remind myself as I walk towards his booth.

Yeah, but none of your other customers ever looked like that.

The closer I get to the booth, the more attractive he becomes. His shocking good looks aren't the product of makeup, camera angles, and flattering lighting, nope, it's all him.

I take in the way his baby blue shirt stretches across his broad shoulders, hugging his biceps and pectoral muscles so well that I just want to take a bite, the top few buttons undone just enough to show off his tight undershirt. Underneath the table, I can see his strong thighs encased in black denim and his expensive leather designer tennis shoes.

I also notice the way his dark chestnut brown hair sweeps away from his forehead, highlighting his straight nose, sharp cheekbones and iron jaw line with just the hint of stubble… the sensual curve of his lips… the piercing slate blue of his eyes…

As they stare right back at me.

His gaze is hot, sensuous, as it travels from my well worn black Converses across the curves of my body, to my face.

Oh, god. Did he really just check me out?

If I didn't know better, by the look in his eye and the upturn of his mouth, I would think he likes what he sees. There's no way.

But still, my mouth goes dry, my nipples pebble tight in my bra. I can feel my core become wet and heavy, clenching tightly in anticipation.

He's the sexiest man I've ever seen, and in that moment, I've never been more turned on in my life.

I can feel my hand shake as I reach into my apron to pull out my order pad. It's that stupid detail that pulls me back into reality.

There's absolutely no way Nathanial Stone thinks I'm attractive. I'm a diner waitress in a podunk town in south Louisiana. This man dates supermodels and movie stars and socialites whose bodies have been carved and honed to perfection.

I'm just me.

I mean, I know I don't break mirrors and there's nothing *wrong* with how I look, but I'm also realistic enough to know that I'm nowhere near as polished and stylized as the women pictured beside him on the front cover of every supermarket gossip magazine in America.

Besides, he's probably just in town for a short visit and will be gone soon, anyway. Plus, I learned my lesson years ago with Brady not to jump into bed too soon. I mean, really, it's not like anything is going to happen between us, and it's absurd to think that anything would. He's him and I'm me.

What I'm probably seeing on his face is hunger. For food.

Strangely enough, that realization calms me right down, which is a good thing, given that I'm now at his table and it's time to put on my "work smile" and talk.

"Hi, I'm Tori and I'm taking over for Elizabeth. I see you already have coffee, is there anything else I can get you, sir?"

FIVE

Nate

Your pussy.

I bite my tongue to stop myself from saying that out loud. The open candor in her gaze gives me the feeling that responding "I want to eat your pussy" would not make the best first impression on her. But as my eyes drift down to the hard press of her nipples beading against her sweater, I wonder if maybe it would be received well.

Best to play it safe and not risk ruining any chance I have with that delicious body, I think as my gaze travels across the lush flare of her hips to the juncture between her soft thighs, hidden beneath her cheerful red apron and the thin fabric of her tight leggings. *Definitely a body made to be fucked.*

My strong reaction to her voluptuous curves is somewhat surprising to me. But, then again, maybe not. Being in the film industry has limited my exposure to only women with a very specific body type. Before that flood of picture-perfect bodies, I was attracted to all shapes and sizes, with no real preference.

I can't shake the image of burying my head between this woman's—*Tori's*—thighs as she's tied to my bed. Red rope would be beautiful against her creamy skin.

It's quite clear from the way I start to harden in my jeans that I have a type. And she's it. *I wonder what her thoughts are on bondage...*

She's still waiting for an answer to her food question and the one I want to give is probably not the answer she's looking for.

I take an extra moment to admire her striking features from close up. She's naturally beautiful in a way that I'm unused to, and I'm quite certain that she has no clue. It's refreshing in a way few things are nowadays.

My eyes go back to her nipples and the way they push against her green sweater. I'm wondering if they're a dusky rose or a darker pink, like...

"Cherries."

"I'm sorry?" Tori questions, her head tilting to the side. Her confused expression is adorable. It makes me wonder if she's as open and easy to read when she's being fucked into oblivion.

"Do you have anything made with cherries?" I tease, my top teeth scraping along my bottom lip as my eyes wander back down to her breasts.

This time she's aware of where my eyes linger.

Color floods her cheeks and she averts her gaze, her plump lip caught between her teeth. She's beautiful.

She's also really uncomfortable.

"I didn't mean to embarrass you," I soothe. Her not-quite-green-not-quite-golden gaze drifts back to me, her expression a mix of confusion and uncertainty, her dilated pupils telling me she's just as turned on as I am. "I just have a craving."

She chews on her lip again, looking down, enhancing the soft curve of her neck, unintentionally becoming the perfect image of submission, and I can feel my cock jump in response. Under the table, I press my palm against my growing hardness, trying to gain control of myself.

Not the time, not the place. Not yet.

"Cherry pie. Please," I finally answer her question, mildly disappointed when she hurries away from my table.

I'll be in town for awhile, though. I'll have plenty of time to find out if her pussy is the same color as her mouth. In fact, I look forward to it.

SIX

Nate

The bell above the door rings for the five thousandth time this week, distracting me from the succulent rise and fall of Tori's ass as she walks away from me. The vinyl cushion of this booth has had my ass-print permanently indented into it over the past six days.

The cable company refused to get off their collective asses and install my internet for *days*. Then, when they finally did get around to sending someone, I discovered that I actually preferred setting camp up in the diner over working alone in the silence of my rented house. At least here, I can have a constant supply of coffee and cherry pie delivered by the sweetest waitress this side of the Mississippi. And she has a fantastic ass that provides an excellent distraction from script breakdowns and budgets and shooting schedules.

Out of the corner of my eye I see Elizabeth enter the restaurant again. She's followed by someone smaller, a boy who's maybe eight or nine years old.

I don't think much of it until the boy glances my way. My breath stops in my chest.

Even across the restaurant I recognize those blue eyes. They're the same ones that look at me from my mirror every morning. The same silver blue that I share with my brothers and my father.

Holy shit.

If I didn't know better, I'd think that I had a child. But I know he's not mine.

He's my brother's.

I study the little boy closer. He has the same lanky build as Chance, the same milk chocolate brown hair, the same cleft in his chin.

I'm an uncle.

I sit back in my seat, shocked by the revelation that I'm learning—eight, nine?—years too late. I look to Elizabeth, hoping to have some sign that maybe I'm misinterpreting things, that maybe it's a huge coincidence.

But I can tell by the tight draw of her lips and the sudden pallor of her skin as she meets my gaze that I'm not wrong. I have a nephew.

I'm hit by a wave of disappointment in my brother. I can't believe he never told me. Even worse, I can't believe he left Elizabeth here alone with his child to take care of while he went off to chase his dreams.

No wonder she didn't stay in Chicago. She had a child to raise.

Elizabeth sits the boy at the lunch counter and helps him fish out his homework from his backpack. After settling him in with a glass of water and a tender kiss on his hair, she comes back to my table.

"His name is Benji. Benji David St. Clair," she confirms, sliding into the booth.

Hot rage engulfs me, directed straight at my irresponsible younger brother. This is just like him to walk away from his obligations. He's always been one to ignore things he doesn't want to deal with, so I'm not shocked in the slightest that he never told us he had a kid.

He knows that Leo and I would have ended his run at fame and fortune in a hot minute if we knew he had a child back home. We would have dragged him back to Louisiana by his hair if needed. It's one thing to be a penniless struggling artist trying to follow your dream if you're single and childless, it's completely selfish and irresponsible to do it if you have a child to help raise.

Our father may be a bastard, but our mother raised us better than that.

"I'm going to kill Chance," I fume. "Does he help you at all? Pay child support?" I ask as I reach into my back pocket for my wallet. I'm readjusting my finances in my head, moving money around to set up a trust to support my nephew, figuring out how much to write the first check for, while coming up with a plan to take a few days off to meet up with Chance and beat some sense into him.

I pull out my check book and a pen, ready to write, when Elizabeth interrupts me, "I don't want your money."

"It's not for you, it's for Benji. He's my nephew and I'm going to take care of him since my brother hasn't," I insist, filling out the check and wondering how much is a good starting point— ten thousand? Twenty?

How does money make up for lost years without your family? Without your father?

Goddamned fucking Chance.

"Chance doesn't know."

I pause writing to look up at her. She's tense, eyes averted. Guilty. "What do you mean he doesn't know?"

"I never told him," she whispers, shamefaced.

"Why not?" I ask, finishing the check and handing it to her.

She tries pushing it back to me, "I can't take that. It's too much."

"It's for Benji. Put it in a savings account for college if nothing else. Think of it as… eight?" She nods. "Eight years of missed Christmas and birthday presents."

"We do fine here," she protests. "We're not rich but we get by. I don't need your money."

"I know. You're doing a great job. Let me be an uncle," I insist. I don't know why taking care of Benji means so much to me, why I'm insisting she take the sizeable check. Maybe it's because I know what it's like to be a kid and not having anyone to rely on except for an abusive alcoholic dad. "Let me help take care of Benji."

She nods shakily, taking the check. She gasps when she sees the number. It's enough for at least a semester at a private university; it might even cover all four years if he ends up at an in-state school. I still don't think it's enough to make up for years of negligence on my part, but it's a start.

"You don't have to pay me to see him," she says, trying to push the check back to me. "I wouldn't keep him from you. Not anymore, now that you know he exists."

"I'm not bribing you to let me get to know him," I stop her. "I want to help you, so let me. Eight missed Christmases and birthdays, Elizabeth."

She relents, sliding the check into her pocket.

"So why haven't you told my brother?" I ask again.

"Do you think he would have left Boden if he knew?"

"Chance? Probably," I reply bluntly. "He's my brother and I love him, but he's never in his life taken responsibility seriously."

She gives me a sad smile, almost as if she's sad *for* me. "See, the Chance I got to know that summer was different. He matured a lot, working here, having my parents give him some stability, having the opportunity to step out of the shadows left by you and Leo and even little Felix. I'm sorry that you never saw that side of him. But he loved me and I think, at the time, he was looking for a reason to stay. I chose not to give him one."

She sighs, sitting back in the booth, "We both know that he was bigger than Boden. He never belonged here."

"And you do?" I ask. "You were leaving too. You were going to Chicago for art school."

"How do you know that?" she questions. But when she meets my gaze I know she has her answer: Chance told me.

She breaks eye contact, her gaze going to her son sitting on the high stool at the lunch counter, kicking his dangling feet in childish innocence. Her expression says that her whole world revolves around Benji.

"Some things are bigger than art school," she finally replies, turning back to me. "I'm happy with my decision. Benji is happy. And you said that Chance is happy."

I give a slight nod, feeling a pang of guilt for lying to her about that. For all that he fakes it, my brother hasn't been happy in a long time.

"Would you like to meet him?" The question tears me from my distracted thoughts. I'm pretty sure Elizabeth can tell that I wasn't focused.

"Benji," she says with a smile. "Would you like to meet your nephew?"

"Absolutely," I reply.

A rare twinge of nervousness hits me. It feels like everything is about to change. I know he's just a kid, but after growing up with only my brothers to rely on, family is important to me.

Elizabeth calls Benji over and he jumps off the chair, arms outstretched like he's flying. I can tell the kid has a lot of energy. He probably has to be constantly moving, just like Chance.

It's strange to see a miniaturized version of my brother walking towards me. He even has the same rangy saunter my brother has, which is downright weird to see on an eight-year-old.

"Looks just like Chance, doesn't he?" Elizabeth whispers, eyebrow raised, a small grin tilting up the corner of her mouth.

"Downright eerie," I remark, though as Benji gets closer, I can see the subtle differences in features, like how he has Elizabeth's smattering of freckles across his nose and the way his hair is more curly than wavy.

Still. It's obvious that he's family.

Elizabeth slips out of the booth and takes Benji's hand once he's close, bending down to be at his height. She doesn't have far to lean, the kid apparently has Chance's height as well, which is probably a good thing since Elizabeth is so short.

"Benji, this is your Uncle Nate," she says, "He's going to be in town for awhile. He's one of your dad's brothers."

The boy nods solemnly before turning to me.

"Do you play music too?" he asks, holding his hand out to shake.

I can't help but look at Elizabeth at this, noting her amused, affectionate smile directed at her son's precocious gesture.

"No, I don't play music. I work in movies."

Benji nods somberly, a near spitting image of my oldest brother Leo, and it takes a lot to hold in my laugh.

"That's cool, too, I guess," Benji replies. "My dad plays music and sings in a really important band, so I don't get to see him."

I want to tell him that that's going to change soon, but it's not my place to be making promises, so instead I comment, "That's a bummer."

Benji shrugs, probably not knowing what to say to that. Elizabeth takes the moment to jump in. "I have to get back to work and Benji probably has homework to finish...?" Benji nods, shoulders slumping in disappointment. "So if you want to say goodbye to Uncle Nate—"

"Want to do homework over here?" The words fall out of my mouth, interrupting Elizabeth. "If that's OK with your mom?" I ask, looking to Elizabeth for her blessing.

"Can I?" Benji asks his mom, wide eyed. The boy thrums with ill-concealed excitement.

"He's not going to bother you?" she asks.

"Nah, we can do our homework together," I grin, with a wink to my excited nephew.

"Adults have homework too?" he grimaces, horrified.

"We do!" I joke back.

"Homework sucks," he scowls.

"Benji David! Watch your language," Elizabeth scolds.

"Yes, ma'am," he pouts, chewing on his lip and stubbing his toe on the ground.

"Go get your stuff, kid, and join me," I say.

Benji's eyes light up right before he dashes across the room. Elizabeth follows slowly behind him, ready to give him a hand with his things.

He's back within moments, second grade workbooks in hand, ready to go. Once he's settled, I lean forward and whisper to him, "You're right, you know."

"'Bout what?" His bright eyes shine.

"Homework sucks."

Gleeful giggles erupt from the boy, the sight warming a cold dark spot in my heart that I didn't know existed.

I've never given much thought to children one way or another. They just kind of existed separate from me and occasionally we'd come into contact, usually when they were misbehaving. But this one?

This one I like.

"What are you two giggling about?" Elizabeth asks, mock serious, as she drops Benji's backpack off at the table. "Are you two getting into trouble already?"

"I'm just agreeing with my nephew," I grin at her.

"About what?"

I glance at Benji, his joyful eyes wide over the hands he has clapped over his mouth to keep his laughter inside. I wink at him.

"Homework."

~~~~~~

Benji calms down soon after Elizabeth gets called to take care of another table, and I'm able to get back to answering the flood of people asking for my opinion on different aspects of this film. Producers, actors, set designers, casting directors, studio heads... each one pressuring me to answer their urgent-to-them questions and make decisions yesterday.

The producers are already worried about being behind schedule even though everything appears to be actually two weeks ahead of what I had budgeted for. The actors have character question after character question, which would be great except that I answered those questions with them, in person, before I flew out here. The set designers are asking me about my preference for eggplant versus aubergine, which I thought were the same color but apparently there's a subtle difference that somehow matters. The casting directors have a growing list of audition videos for me to watch, which I'll be happy to get to *once I have time*, and the studio execs want me to cast my psychotic ex in one of the main roles, which, fuck no.

It's crazy how much work and people and decisions and *bullshit* go into making a movie.

I'm loving every fucking minute of it. I'm in my element, making decisions, telling people what to do and how to do it, controlling every minute detail that goes into making an excellent film.

It's a dominant's dream and I'm fucking fantastic at it.

~~~~~~

I look up from my computer, cracking my back and ready to take a break. Benji is diligently coloring on some handout, his tongue sticking out the side of his mouth in concentration. Hilarious.

My coffee's cold by now and I realize that with all the ruckus over meeting my nephew, I never got my daily slice of cherry pie that I ordered from Tori when I first arrived.

Elizabeth is across the room, talking to some old couple in the corner booth, but Tori is available. She's staring right at me, in fact.

Caught you, I think as our eyes meet.

A delicious blush blossoms on her cheeks as I grin at her, quirking my eyebrow and letting her know that I know that she was staring at me. She tears her gaze away, blushing harder, biting her lip in embarrassment.

I'd feel bad for making her feel self-conscious except that she's fucking captivating like this.

I raise my coffee cup at her. I wouldn't think it's possible for someone to blush even more, but she does. Her bashfulness is really rather endearing. Makes me wonder what else she's shy about.

Will she be too shy to beg me to fuck her or will she demand to be taken?

I have a feeling it will be a little bit of both.

She arrives at my table and refills my cup, carefully avoiding making eye contact with me.

"Is there anything else I can get you?" she asks my right shoulder.

"I believe I'm missing my pie."

This time, her wide eyes meet mine in horror as she winces at her mistake.

"Oh god, I forgot," she breathes miserably. "Cherry, right?"

I nod, intrigued by the play of emotions on her face. It's as if I can see every thought she has in Technicolor display across her face. It's fascinating to watch.

"Would you like anything else with it? Ice cream?"

"Can I have ice cream and pie, Auntie Tori?" Benji chimes in, looking up from his coloring with wide-eyed anticipation.

"Yeah, Auntie Tori," I grin. "Can we have ice cream and pie?"

Tori pauses, looking between us both before searching the restaurant for Elizabeth, who must be in the back.

"Have you had your snack today?" Tori asks the boy, chewing on her lip in indecision.

He rolls his eyes. "No, Auntie Tori. And I promise to eat my vegetables for dinner tonight, too."

Benji turns to me and solemnly says, "Mommy and Auntie Tori won't let us have pie and ice cream unless we eat our vegetables, Uncle Nate."

"Well then." I turn to 'Auntie Tori'. "I solemnly swear to eat my vegetables tonight. Even if it's Brussels sprouts."

Tori nods, eyes flashing with mirth, "Alright then. Two slices of cherry pie a la mode coming up."

I watch the luscious sway of her hips as she walks away from us. *That ass.*

I turn to find Benji staring at me, a disturbed expression on his face. "Do you really have to eat Brussels sprouts?"

"Only if I'm having pie," I kid.

"I don't know if even Auntie Tori's pie is worth having to eat *Brussels sprouts.*"

I bite back what I want to say, remembering that the kid is eight. "So, that's Auntie Tori, hmm? I didn't know your mom had a sister."

41

Benji shrugs, and goes back to coloring, methodically choosing the next crayon to use. "She's not my *real* aunt. She just lives with us and helps momma here. But momma says we love her like she's family so she's my auntie."

"That's nice. I don't have an auntie," I tell him, sipping my coffee.

He looks up at me, horrified. "You *don't*? But Auntie Tori is the *best*. She makes the best cakes and pies and she gives the greatest hugs and she... she's just the best auntie *ever*!"

"I'm sure she is," I reply, touched by how much he loves his surrogate aunt.

But that doesn't seem to appease him as he frowns down at the table.

"Something bothering you, buddy?" I ask after a solid minute has passed without Benji saying anything.

The kid finally looks up, brow furrowed. "I think I'm going to have to share Auntie Tori with you so you can have an auntie too."

Before I can reply, Tori interrupts us, sliding the plates of warm cherry pie and vanilla ice cream in front of us. Though she actively avoids looking at me, it's hard not to notice how down Benji seems.

"You OK, Benji?" she asks, finally glancing at me, trying to see if I know what's going on.

"Benji just offered to share you with me," I tell her, enjoying the way color floods her cheeks all over again right before she tears her eyes from me to look back at her 'nephew'.

"Uncle Nate doesn't have an auntie and I told him that you're the best," Benji explains. "Can you be his auntie too?"

"Oh, um, wow," she stammers, blushing harder with every second, "Thanks, Benji. But don't you think Uncle Nate is old enough not to need an auntie?"

Benji gasps, absolutely horrified. "You can be too old for aunties? I'm going to lose you?"

I can see the kid is about to lose it and I don't know what to do, besides looking for his mother, who's conspicuously missing from the dining room.

"Oh, no, sweetheart," Tori croons, pulling him into a hug. "That's not what I meant. I just thought Uncle Nate would be too old to *want* me as an auntie." Her eyes meet mine with a panicked request for help.

"I'd love to share Auntie Tori with you, bud, as long as Auntie Tori is OK with it," I grin, ignoring the glare Tori throws at me over Benji's head.

"You don't mind, do you, Auntie Tori?" Benji pleads.

"If you don't mind, I don't mind," she relents.

It's hard to keep from laughing, and from the way she shakes her head and rolls her eyes at me, I can tell that my amusement is just annoying her more.

She's delightful.

She gets waved over to another table and with a kiss to Benji's hair, she's gone, hips swaying, ass looking good enough to eat.

Yeah, she's fucking delightful, all right.

~~~~~~

I spend the rest of the afternoon working, watching Tori interact with her customers during my breaks. There's something about her that I find mesmerizing. It's in the graceful movements of her steps, the unrestrained emotions that play across her face.

I'm an actor—displaying emotions and showing people how my character feels is the reason why I have a fortune in the bank. I work with the best in the business, actresses who can cry on command, actors who can get a whole theater laughing with just a look. But it's not real.

When I watch Tori, when I watch the emotions flicker across her face, open and unrestrained, I see more. She's honest in the simplicity, in the ease of what she feels.

I see kindness in the way she reads the menu to the old man whose vision is barely there, generosity when she slips an upset child a fresh cookie, and integrity when she pays for it at the register from her own tips.

There's something about her that I can't quite put my finger on, but I know that I've never met anyone like her.

She's definitely nothing like the last woman I was seriously involved with. Tori smiles with her whole face, her eyes alight with laughter after one of her customers tells her a joke.

The last woman I was with only smiled if there were cameras nearby to capture it. That's one of the many reasons why I ended things between us before I came out here. What we had was dysfunctional even on a good day. In fact, part of the reason why I came out here early was to get away from her.

That sobering thought reminds me that I came to Louisiana to work, not to sleep with the locals.

~~~~~~~

The next time I look up, it's nearing closing time. Benji and Elizabeth are long gone, and Tori is left in charge of the diner. I follow her with my eyes, watching the way her full breasts push against her shirt as she wipes down the last table in the restaurant.

She glances at the clock on the wall and then at me. I know it's time for me to leave so she can close up for the night and go home, but something's keeping me in my seat, some need to have her walk over and acknowledge me.

It's when I'm watching her plump lips telling me the diner is closing, imagining them wrapped around my cock as her bright eyes look up at me, her hands cuffed behind her back, that I think:

Mine.

Fuck.

SEVEN

Nate

The Finewhile Diner officially becomes my office. It's not for the greasy food or the solid cup of coffee. It's not for the free Wi-Fi and definitely not for the lack of distractions. In the rental house the studio arranged for me, I have a distraction-free office and a high tech gourmet espresso machine that can probably do everything but navigate the space shuttle. I can watch audition reels in the small private cinema that the studio installed in the spare guest room rather than watching on a fifteen inch MacBook Pro through wireless Bose headphones inside a busy diner.

There are a thousand reasons why I should be working from home, but every day I find myself stepping into the diner, the same little bell ringing overhead as Tori turns to greet me with a smile and a blushing "Good morning."

In the breaks between putting out pre-production fires, casting actors, hiring crew, and talking and emailing with the producers, agents, attorneys, and crew necessary to make a multi-million dollar motion picture, I watch her. I'm not blatantly staring and it's not intended to be weird and creepy. My eyes unintentionally seek her out between bites of club sandwich and

46

sips from my umpteenth cup of coffee. I've never before felt the need to just sit and watch a woman, so this gravitational pull to her is new for me. I don't know how to make it stop and I don't know if I even want to.

She's a natural submissive and she doesn't have a clue.

"Try to be more obvious, why don't you?" Elizabeth says behind me as she reaches around to refill my cup. "Don't even try to deny it. You haven't stopped staring at her once. If you weren't so damn attractive, it'd be creepy."

"Does she know?" I ask.

"She knows lots of things, Nate. You'll have to be a bit more specific," Elizabeth says, sliding into the booth.

"You know," I hint.

Her eyes narrow as she stares me down, trying to decide if we're thinking about the same thing.

"If you're talking about the sex stuff, no," she spits out. "I try to keep my private life behind closed doors, thank you. Obviously, Chance can't keep his fat mouth shut."

"He was—"

"Drunk," she interrupts bitterly. "I'm starting to notice a pattern."

She's right. It was after another one of my brother's benders that he confessed about the more private parts of his relationship with Elizabeth, about how they dabbled in BDSM over that summer. About how by the end of the summer, she was his submissive as much as she was his girlfriend. And how they switched, when the need arose.

"Do you still play?" I ask directly. There's no reason to beat around the bush.

She coldly stares me down and for a second I think that she might throw her coffee carafe at me, but then she sighs and rolls her eyes as she answers, "Occasionally. There's a club in the Quarter that I go to when the mood strikes me. *La Petite Mort*. It's discreet, exclusive. There are a lot of people in town who would be unhappy if it got out that they're a regular. You need a recommendation from a member if you want to get through the door. But let me know and I can get you one." She smirks. "I've become rather notorious for my expertise with a crop."

She pauses and once again I'm trapped under her piercing stare. I don't know how this woman didn't eat my brother alive. "Don't get it in that pretty head of yours that I'll be your plus one, though. One Stone boy in a lifetime is my quota."

"Chance would murder me and leave my body in the bayou for the alligators if I even tried," I reply.

"Right," Elizabeth murmurs, biting back a hint of a smile. "I think it's time for me to get back to work."

My eyes drift over to Tori as she steps out of the kitchen with a tray of food for a table of men just off shift from the refinery. One of them says something and a blush stains her cheeks as she looks down.

"Does she know what she is?" I ask.

Elizabeth follows my gaze to Tori. I can tell that she sees what I see: Tori's natural submission. "There's been no one to show her."

"Are you going to warn me away?" I challenge. At this point, I think there is very little that would keep me from pursuing Tori.

"Do I need to?" she counters. "Tori may be living in a small backwoods town, but she's smart and kind and bigger than Boden... both the town and the jackass who brought her here. I read the tabloids. I see the trash you bring home. You'd be *lucky* to land Tori."

~~~~~~

It's late and Elizabeth has long gone home with Benji when I finally have a moment alone with Tori.

"Go out with me."

EIGHT

Tori

"Go out with me."

...

...

...

...

My brain stalls. I must have misheard him, there's no other explanation. But he's looking at me as if he's expecting an answer. Is he serious? Is he messing with me? Am I hallucinating? This has to be a joke, right? I've seen the tabloids, I know what kind of women he dates, and roadside diner waitresses from the Louisiana bayous are not it.

It would be so easy to say yes, it feels natural to try to please him.

"No," I decide. I don't trust him. I don't trust his motivations. No matter how hot he is, it's not worth this much turmoil (or the potential heartbreak when he inevitably leaves). "Is there anything else I can get you?"

Nate leans back in his chair, obviously surprised. I'm sure he's not used to people telling him no, much less women. Yeah, I've made the right decision.

The thing is, every time I see him after that night, he asks me again. Nothing has changed. I still don't trust him or his motivations. So I keep telling him no.

It's the third night that he asks me, "Why?"

It's been a long day and I'm tired, my feet hurt, and I'm wearing a strawberry shake that I spilled all over myself seven hours ago after a customer slammed into me. I don't have the time or the patience for playing games. "Why does it matter?"

"Because I'm trying to get to know you better and dinner is the first step," he candidly replies.

"Why do you want to get to know me better? Aren't there waitresses in Hollywood?" I ask the next night after I tell him no while dropping the bill off at his table.

"You're more than your job," he counters, looking down to sign his credit card receipt. "For example, you're an exceptional baker, and maybe I really like pie."

It's hard to hold back my laughter as I walk away.

The next night, I have to ask, "Is it the challenge? Has no one ever told you 'no' before?"

He chuckles and lounges back in the booth, blue eyes hooded and dark. "Beautiful, I work in the movie industry. Contrary to popular belief, I get told no every day."

I ignore the thrill at being called beautiful because it sounds like a line. I just don't get him. "There have got to be other women in town who'll go out with you. Why do you keep pushing? What's in it for you?"

I didn't realize I was going to say anything until the questions were already out of my mouth, and now it's too late to take them back.

"Why do you think there are other reasons?" Nate counters. "It's only dinner."

"It's never just dinner. There are always strings attached," I assert.

I walk away.

The next night, he asks, "What are you afraid of?"

Everything.

"I'm not afraid of anything," I lie.

The next night. "Is there someone else? Is that the problem?"

"Do you respect another man's claim on me more than you respect me?" I challenge.

"Absolutely not. We both are well aware that you're your own woman. But it would explain why you won't join me for dinner," he replies, capturing my wrist in his warm hand, his thumb rubbing soothing patterns across my racing pulse.

"Why won't you accept that maybe I just don't want you?" I snap, futilely trying to pull my hand from his grasp, trying to deny the rush of heat pulsing through me at my temporary helplessness.

He gives me a wolfish grin, like he knows exactly what I'm feeling, before releasing me from his iron grip. "Because, beautiful, we both know that's a lie."

~~~~~~

That night I lie awake in bed, my body aching for something I barely understand. I know what he says is true. I want him more than I want air to breathe.

I look at him and my body reacts in a way that it never has before, even in the throes of passion. I look at him and I start aching so deep inside it takes all I can to think, to breathe, to speak. He's like the brightest flame and it takes everything in me to resist its call.

I know that if I give in, I'll get burned so deeply, there might be nothing left once I come out the other side.

But, god, I want to step into that flame.

I can't do this anymore.

So the next night when he asks, I rage, "Do you not understand the word *no*? What will it take for you to respect that I mean what I say? Why will you not take no for an answer? What will it take for you to stop?"

I can tell even in my fury that I surprised him. He wasn't expecting this level of animosity from me. There's a distant, disconnected part of me as I'm screaming at him in the empty diner that is shocked by the anger, too. It's as if with those words I'm funneling all my fury at the world—the bad breaks and missed opportunities, Brady and my mom—at the handsome, successful man in front of me who merely wants to take me to dinner.

So it shocks me when he breaks the silence after I've finished screaming to say, "You're right. I apologize."

I don't know what to say. It's the last reaction I expected. And so I can't help but stare at him dumbfounded as he packs up his work, pays his bill in cash, and stands up to leave.

I follow him out the door with my eyes, more confused than ever how simple and yet painful it was to get him to go away.

He pushes the door open and stops. There's a pregnant pause before he speaks.

"If you change your mind," he grinds out between his teeth, "you know where to find me. It's a small town."

Then he's gone.

But nothing beats the gnawing knot in my gut as I watch his car back out of the parking lot. Who knew that getting your way would hurt so much?

Why did I say no, again? Because I'm scared of getting hurt?

Too late.

I try to tell myself that I got what I want. He left me alone. It's probably for the best. He's going to be going back to California in a few months anyway. It's not like anything with him would be for the long term.

I can't help but sigh and call myself a moron. After all, he was only proposing dinner, not marriage.

~~~~~~

It's an hour before I finish cleaning up and counting the register. I give the clean kitchen one last glance as I untie my apron, rolling my shoulders after a long, bizarre, painful day. My head's been going back and forth nonstop since Nate left the diner.

On one hand, I completely stand by my decision not to complicate my life any more than it already is.

On the other hand, it's Nate fucking Stone and my knees get weak just from looking at him. And the little voice in the back of my head is telling me that Nate Stone is a man you complicate your life for.

So I go back and forth feeling like the smartest woman alive and a complete and utter idiot.

I'm in smartest-woman-alive-land when I hear the door bell jingle behind me.

The door that is supposed to be locked.

I forgot to lock it.

I go cold. The hair on my arms stands up. Dear lord, I'm about to be robbed.

I say a little prayer that that's all that's going to happen.

"The diner's closed," my voice wavers.

I wait for an answer, hoping with every fiber in my being that maybe, just maybe, it's Elizabeth. Or Nate.

However, I know Elizabeth is home with Benji. So hopefully it's Nate and he just forgot something... though I didn't find anything when I was cleaning up. But there's no contest if the choice is between Nate and a rapist-slash-robber. I'll gladly get naked and throw myself at him.

I roll my eyes at myself, taking a deep breath and telling myself that I'm being ridiculous. It's probably some guy from the refinery wanting a late night meal and he forgot our hours. I grab a knife anyway.

With another deep breath (and grasping the knife tighter), I step through the kitchen doors into the restaurant.

It's not a robber.

It's not Nate either.

"Brady? What are you doing in here? You know we're closed," I hiss at my ex, putting the knife down on the counter.

He leans against the counter, all nonchalant, like he owns the place and hasn't just committed felony breaking and entering. I have to admit, Brady Boden is not hard on the eyes, even after I've had first-hand experience with how hard he is on the heart.

He's blond and blue-eyed with a devilish smirk, a scruffy jawline, and a body that's still hard from his years playing football. He might be a little softer around the middle than he was when I first met him, but, as half the parish can attest, he's still hot enough that most women wouldn't kick him out of bed.

There are some wilting grocery-store-dyed carnations on the counter beside him that he probably got for me, which would be sweet, I guess, except that I've told him multiple times over the past four years that I've known him that dyed carnations are my least favorite flower ever. The ungrateful thought makes me feel like a bitch, but—seriously? —he finally decides to bring me flowers and those are the ones he goes with?

Still, it's a lovely gesture and I can feel myself softening towards him. Even if they are dyed carnations, I love flowers.

"I've been missing you, Tori," Brady drawls, his accent strong enough to be charming, as he holds the flowers out to me. Like a fool, I accept them. "You've been on my mind an awful lot the past few weeks."

"Is that so?" I ask, sniffing the carnations. I don't know why I do it as the sticky sweet scent gets stuck in the back of my throat.

"Yeah, sugar, I've been thinking about that time when I took you up to Natchez and we got that room at the casino up there. We sure did have a good time then, didn't we?"

"Yeah, it was fun, I guess," I reply.

It really was a good weekend. Well, until I ended up with food poisoning from some bad oysters from the buffet and Brady disappeared for the eight hours I was hugging the toilet. But the before and after were great. He bought me a new dress and introduced me to the high rollers in the Players Club, and it felt just like when we started dating back at LSU when I was so proud to be on his arm. I thought he was going to propose that weekend and I was ready to say yes.

"You know, I heard from Big Tony last week, his wife's about to have another baby," Brady continues. "I think this is gonna be their third one in three years, lucky S.O.B."

"It feels like they just got married," I comment. "They had a beautiful wedding."

"It sure was a fancy shindig, wasn't it?"

"It was perfect," I sigh, lost in the memory of soaring ceilings, white roses, and phenomenal food.

Big Tony was one of Brady's teammates from LSU and had just finished his rookie season with the Dallas Cowboys as an offensive lineman when he and his college girlfriend Moira got married at the Cowboys Golf Club. It was both amazing and intimidating brushing shoulders with celebrity athletes... until Brady went and ruined the night by drunkenly picking a fight with Brandon Weedon, the freaking *quarterback* for the Dallas Cowboys.

Walking behind Brady with all of our stuff as he was forcibly removed by the club's security makes the top three in the list of my mortifying moments.

That's the thing with Brady—when it was good, it was great, but when it was bad, it was exceptionally terrible. That's what makes it so hard in the in-between when I'm tired and lonely and just want to be loved. I start to forget the bad and only remember the good and the great. I forget that when I was in the midst of the good and the great, I ignored or excused the bad and the terrible until something happened that was so unforgivable that I finally would get fed up and leave.

I think that's why I'm so scared that I'm going to wake up married to Brady with three kids and no love or respect. I know how easy it is to be pulled in by his charm and his pretty words, the empty gestures and false promises until the feelings happen, feelings that lead to bad judgment and bad decisions and lots of heartache and self-recriminations. I know all of this, I know what a bad decision this man is, but I also know how easy it is to backslide into a false sense of security fortified by a silver tongued snake.

"I was just thinking, babe, that we haven't gone out in a few months," he grins. "Why is that?"

For a split second, I'm drawn in by his deep voice and charming smile, but then I think about the question and remember the answer. It takes everything in me not to roll my eyes.

"I think her name was Darlene. Or was it Tammy? Wait, no. Tammy was before Darlene but after Lanée. I remember *that* because Lanée was the one who gave you the crabs that wouldn't go away. So no, Brady, I have *no clue* why we aren't dating," I muse.

"Oh, sugar," he grins with his best panties-dropping smile. "We both know you forgave me for that. You know you're the one I really want."

Well. I know what a giant stinking pile of garbage *that* is. I've forgiven a lot from our on-again-off-again relationship, but being the laughingstock of the parish is not one of those things.

"Right," I deadpan, tired of the same BS line he fed me for years. "If that's all, I need you to leave. It's late, I'm tired, and it's past time to close up."

I try to walk past him, but he grabs my arm, pulling me to an abrupt, and painful, stop. Yeah, the manhandling is another reason why I'm staying away.

"I hear that Hollywood douchebag has been hanging out here, getting all comfortable like he owns the place," Brady says, inches from my face. His breath smells like stale beer. That explains some things. "I also heard that he seems to be spending a little extra time talking to you. But you know better than to get ideas. You know that even with these silly games you play, you're really mine. Right, babe?"

I'm frozen. I'm blank. I don't think I could respond if I wanted to. I wish I could pull away, but my body won't move.

Brady takes my silence as confirmation and keeps going, his accent becoming stronger, turning grating and uneducated, "I think it's time for you to stop playing these silly games of yours. You had your fun playing like you was a single woman, but it's time to stop. So tomorrow night, I'm gonna pick you up, you're gonna wear one of those tight little numbers I bought you, and we're gonna go down to the bowling alley and you're gonna watch me play with the boys and maybe I'll get you some of that pizza that you like. But not too much. I can't be marrying a fatty."

In that moment, I see my future so clearly. I see myself saying yes and having him pick me up tomorrow forty-five minutes late without a sorry. I'll watch him bowl and get drunk with his friends, while I'm stuck eating stale greasy pizza and hoping to be acknowledged. It'll be the first of many dates just like it. He'll keep sleeping with other women, just like he has every other time I've been stupid enough to date him. But unlike those other times, I'm tired and worn out and just don't care, and he knows it. And when he starts sensing me inevitably getting fed up, he'll start talking about rings and marriage, and I'll be dumb enough to believe he's serious. But he'll hold off because *excuses* until I accidentally get knocked up because I have a sinus infection and my antibiotics messed with my birth control. We'll get married because that's what good Catholic boys do, and I'll go on to have a couple more kids while he screws every woman within fifty miles. And I'll suck it up and just slowly wither away until I'm dead.

Brady's right. It's inevitable. It doesn't matter how hard I fight against it, my future's tied to him. It'll be a lot less painful in the long run to just accept it.

I open my mouth, ready to choke out the words that will tie me to him, but I stop when I remember gorgeous, sexy Nate asking me to dinner, night after night, acting like he wants *me* and not just the idea of me. How he talks *to* me, not *at* me, and how he actually seems to listen to me when I reply. He treats me like a real person and not some pretty accessory that feeds his ego.

I might end up marrying Brady once everything is said and done, but, fuck it, I'm going to have fun first.

"That's not going to work for me, Brady," I reply. "I've got plans tomorrow night."

~~~~~~

Half an hour later, the rush of bravado has dwindled into a roiling pit of butterflies having World War III somewhere around my pancreas.

Nate was right, I do know where he lives. And now I'm standing on his dark porch, wondering if I can get away with turning around and walking home. I mean, I knocked and rang the doorbell. There was no answer. He's probably asleep. A+ for effort.

I turn to leave and the porch light flips on. I freeze. *Noooooooooo.*

The tumblers in the lock are sticking because of the humidity and I know I've got maybe two seconds before the door's open. I wonder if I make a break for the street now... I look desperately at the road behind me. There's no way I'll make it in time. But I take a step off the front porch, because maybe he won't notice the crazy lady running down the street once he gets that door open.

"Tori?" Nate's deep voice is like dark chocolate and sex and all that is right in the world and it stops me in my tracks.

I turn slowly, hating how I can *feel* how incredibly red my face is from blushing, and I just *know* the overhead light is going to make me look like a deranged stop sign.

The sight that greets me makes my mouth go dry, my heart stutter, and my knees stop working. Worst of all, the electric tingling rush that goes through me makes me think that I, for real, may have just had a tiny orgasm.

In the moments it takes me to get my breath back, all I can see is skin. Glorious, glorious, golden tan skin. Acres of it pulled tight across plains of hard muscles lightly dusted with springy dark hair. Never before in my life have I wanted to fall to my knees and worship a man's body, but, god, it's taking everything in me to keep standing.

He must have just gotten out of the shower when I rang the door bell. Rivulets of water stream across warm skin and I'm hit with the fantastic image of running my tongue along their path until he's dry. I follow the trail of one of the droplets as it snakes around his nipple, twisting and writhing until it catches in the deep groove of his oblique, following the shadowed crevasse down, down, down to the open, barely zipped fly. He's pressed hard and thick against the damp denim, the material tightening with his every heartbeat. God, much longer and one small shift will pull the zipper all the way down.

I clench tight with the thought, the zing of pleasure from my deepest place shocking me back to life.

My eyes shoot up to his and I know that I was caught looking. His eyes are blue fire, pinning me in place and so hot and intense that with one word from him I could come. I clench tight on an invisible emptiness and I'm so needy and wet that I think I moan aloud.

If it's even possible, I blush deeper and dry swallow, trying to get my tongue to move and failing. I shut my eyes, hoping to disappear, trying to remember why I'm here...

Right.

"Yes," I croak huskily. "To dinner. Yes."

I turn and run.

NINE

Tori

I've been a bundle of nerves since I ran off Nate's front porch. I can't believe I had the balls to walk up, knock on his door, and tell him yes.

I can't believe how hot that man is when he's half-naked and wet. The way the beading water slipped down plains of golden skin, dampening the worn material of his well-loved jeans before pressing closer to the Promised Land barely hidden behind tight denim and a straining zipper.

Never before have I had such a pressing urge to fall to my knees and pull a zipper tab down with my teeth.

How he hasn't won Sexiest Man Alive every year is a mystery and a crime.

I still don't see how someone that incredibly hot wants to go out with *me*. I mean, I know all my parts are where they should be and I don't break mirrors, but, when push comes to shove, I'm no supermodel. Compared to the women on television, I'm barely more than ordinary. But, for some reason, he doesn't care, so I'm going with it. I'm going to rock this date. I'm going to look hot and I'm going to have a good time. It's only dinner.

I'm going to have a heart attack and die.

Just then, I hear a knock on the door. My voice cracks, "Come in."

Elizabeth pops her head inside and surveys me in my state of panic.

"I had a feeling," she says with a sympathetic smile.

I'm standing here in nothing but my bra and panties, hair sopping wet, no makeup on, the contents of my wardrobe strewn across the room, and Nate is supposed to be here in—I check the clock—twenty-five minutes. I should just cancel.

"I should cancel," I decide.

"Nope," Elizabeth chirps. "I'm not going to let you. You're going."

"He could be a serial killer," I return. "I could go out tonight and never come back."

"I've known Nate since we were kids. He's not a serial killer," she laughs.

"He could be very good at keeping it a secret," I throw out desperately. "It would explain why he wants to go out with a measly diner waitress."

"First, stop putting yourself, me, and my restaurant down," Elizabeth orders. "Second, if he's really a serial killer and he dumps your body in the swamp, you can come back to haunt me and tell me 'I told you so'. Deal?"

"Fine. But there's no way I'll be ready in time. And I have nothing to wear," I argue.

"Yes, you do," she counters, "you have The Dress."

"But…" I hesitate. The Dress is a fabulously flattering deep ruby, body skimming wrap dress with a deep plunge that does amazing things for my boobs and a wide black sash that highlights my curves.

The Dress makes me look like sex. It's the dress to end all dresses. It's perfect. It's so perfect, it's dangerous.

I bought The Dress a year ago at the end of my last go-around with Brady. I knew he was cheating and I had some hare-brained idea that I would wear it and seduce him and he'd finally be faithful and ask me to marry him. So I drove to New Orleans and used a gift card I won in a raffle at Benji's school to buy the perfect dress at a small boutique in One Canal Place. But when I got home and tried The Dress on again, I realized Brady didn't deserve the awesomeness that was me in The Dress. And if he didn't deserve something as simple as the benefits from a dress, then he definitely didn't deserve me in his life. So there's a lot of history behind this red dress of mine.

"Yeah, I think it's time for The Dress to make its debut," I concede. "If there's ever a time to wear The Dress..."

"It's when you're going on a date with a super successful, incredibly sexy Hollywood actor," she finishes.

I glance at the clock—we're now t minus twenty. "There's no way I will be ready in time."

"Yes you will. Put this on." Elizabeth throws my robe at me before hollering, "Benji! We need some help!"

Somehow she's right. With eight-year-old Benji blow drying my hair and Elizabeth applying my makeup, I'm somehow magically dressed and sliding Elizabeth's sparkly black peep toe pumps onto my feet when Nate rings the doorbell.

It's showtime.

TEN

Tori

Nate's driving me to New Orleans in his high-performance Midnight Silver Tesla S and I don't know what to talk about. How do you make conversation with someone who lives in a completely different world from you?

I run my hand across the soft black leather of the upholstery, admiring the sheer luxury of a car that costs more than what I made in the past five years. Through the glass roof above my head, I watch the setting sun paint the sky over Lake Pontchartrain in bright pinks and oranges.

Opera plays softly around us through the hidden surround sound speakers, a soprano trilling a delicate aria about lost love or remorse or something, the notes pure and high and perfect.

"How did you get into opera?" I ask, breaking the silence.

He glances over at me, a soft intimate smile gracing his lips as he explains, "I was working on a historical film last year that's featured around the Vienna Opera house during the 19th century. There's something about the majesty of it all that pulls me in."

"What part did you play? Did you sing?"

His chuckle is rich and warm as he replies, "No. Thankfully for everyone involved, I played the rich Lothario trying to win a chorus girl's attention. My brother's the one with all the singing talent."

"Opera is a lot different than what your brother does," I point out with a smile.

There's warmth in his gaze as he glances over at me. "Yeah, but there's a place for his music too."

Thankfully, that breaks the ice and as we drive deeper into the city, we continue discussing our preferences in music and movies and art. Of course, Nate has a lot more experience and exposure to those things, but with the internet and being so close to a major hotspot of culture, I can hold my own.

"You know, I don't really know much about you," I point out as we enter Kenner, one of the outer suburbs of New Orleans. "You know, outside of you liking opera and what can be found on the tabloid covers."

"You read a lot of tabloid articles about me?" he shoots me a satisfied grin that makes me roll my eyes and laugh.

"No, actually, I don't. I'm kind of busy, you know, having a *job* and a *life*, to keep up with the goings-on of Hollywood heart-throbs," I joke.

"Hey, I have a job!" he laughs.

"Yeah, yeah, looking pretty in front of a camera is just *grueling*," I tease.

"I make it look easy," he shoots me a grin. "Alright, hit me. What do you want to know?"

God, everything. I want to know everything about this beautiful, fascinating man. I don't even know where to start.

"I can ask you anything?" I question, a little surprised by the unrestrained access into his life that he just freely offered.

"I guess so," he grinds out. I suddenly take in the way his knuckles tighten on the steering wheel and the tension in his shoulders—he regrets giving me carte blanche access into his life.

What do I do now?

The silence between us grows, and we're suddenly hitting a traffic jam, slowing to a standstill. How do I break the tension? What do I say? What is an easy, stress-free topic?

"What's your favorite holiday?" I throw out, desperate to cut through the growing distance between us.

It's the right move. His hands loosen on the steering wheel, his shoulders relax. It's like I can feel the audible breath from his lips seep into my chest and circle my heart, warming something up deep within me, in a place I didn't know existed, making me feel calm and needed and valuable.

I did that.

He gives a soft chuckle, almost as if he's laughing at himself before replying, "Easy. Thanksgiving. The food. I fucking love the food."

I laugh with him, the tension in the car completely broken with that statement, and for the first time tonight, I think that everything is going to be alright.

"What about you?" he asks. "What's your favorite? Let me guess…"

He studies me out of the corner of his eye once we're at a standstill on the interstate. I can't resist raising my eyebrow right back at him. This'll be good.

He begins, "It's either something very clichéd and romantic like Christmas or Valentine's Day—"

"Why? Because I seem clichéd and romantic to you?" I interrupt, completely teasing, wanting to throw him off just a tiny bit like he does for me.

"No, because you're sweet and sentimental, just like those holidays." He glances over to check my reaction. "That's a compliment, by the way."

"Well you're wrong, it's neither of those."

"Well if you hadn't cut me off, I was going to say that it could also be something more esoteric and unpopular like Labor Day. So which is it?"

I look away from him, studying the family in the SUV beside us, not wanting to answer the question because it's kind of embarrassing now. The silence stretches between us and I think I might just get away with not answering him when:

"I was right. It's Labor Day, isn't it?" he comments, humor ripe in his voice. "What's the reason? It's lonely and unpopular and you felt the need to adopt it?"

Yeah, I'm not answering that.

"Come on, beautiful," he chortles. "Now you have to tell me. It's Labor Day, isn't it?"

"Maybe," I pout. I can't believe that he figured out that I'm the only weirdo in the world who chooses *Labor Day* as their favorite holiday.

"Do you also have a menagerie of stray animals that you've adopted?" he kids.

"Elizabeth's allergic," I sigh. Because, yeah, I'd totally have a houseful of animals if I could. *How does he know this?!*

"I bet you volunteer at the local humane society, don't you?"

Ok, this is just getting unfair.

"No," I lie. He's enjoying this way too much.

"Really? No adopt-a-day events? Petting the puppies?"

I roll my eyes before answering, "Fine. I run the volunteer community outreach program."

He laughs, a full-on belly-aching chortle. He's definitely getting too much amusement out of this.

"What? That too sweet and sentimental for you?" I counter.

"Not at all," he laughs. He shoots me a beautiful grin and my heart swoops into my belly and pops like a confetti-filled balloon.

He continues, with a rueful side-eye, "I may or may not volunteer at SPCALA when I have free time."

"Oh, really? And you were giving me crap for liking animals?" I point out, trying and failing to hide my smile.

"Who doesn't like animals?" he shrugs.

"That's what I say! How can you say no to their cute little faces?"

We're soon driving into downtown, approaching the towering, bulbous Superdome that became infamous during the tragedy of Hurricane Katrina. I take a moment to admire the view as a phenomenal tenor sings a famous aria that I actually recognize.

I start to get nervous when I realize that we're almost at the end of our journey and the actual date-date-where-we're-in-public part of the evening will start. My mouth goes dry and my hands get clammy, and I think that maybe if I keep the light banter going, I'll forget to be nervous and just keep enjoying my time with Nate.

"OK. So your favorite holiday is Thanksgiving, because food, which I approve of," I joke, trying to keep it light, and from his half-smile, I think I'm successful until I ask, "So, then, what's your least favorite holiday?"

The last word is barely out of my mouth when suddenly I realize I may have said something wrong. It's like an ice flow has crashed through the car, and I don't know what to do or how I caused it. I almost think he's not going to answer and I'm scrambling for a way to save the moment and bail us out of this tsunami of tension when a single word falls from his lips.

"Halloween."

I'm aware of the tension, god, it's so palpable I can feel it like I can feel my dress or the leather of the car seats, but, still, stupid me, I press on and try to break it up.

"Don't like candy? Or the costumes? I'd think with all your acting, Halloween would be your fav—"

He cuts me off. "My mom died on Halloween."

Oh no.

"I don't talk about it. It's not publicized. She and dad went into the city. Dad drove them home drunk and hit a big wheeler. He was fine. Mom wasn't."

"Oh god," the words fall from my mouth. "I…"

I stop talking. There's nothing I can say that will make his pain better or fix my gaffe. I did not mean for this to happen.

"It happened," he says, dismissive. "It was horrible, but it happened when I was twelve. I've been alive longer without her than I was with her. I won't say I moved on, but I survived. Her death led to a couple years of hell and misery living with my father, but I got out of Boden. I got away from my dad and I went to L.A. and became a big star." His words have an acidic twist on them. "We all got away. That's what matters."

"But now you're back."

"Now I'm back," he says, tone neutral. I don't know how he feels about that, but the way he said it makes me think it's not too good.

"I hope it's not all bad."

He brakes at a light on Canal Street and looks over at me, his face inscrutable until, slowly, a small smile tugs at the corner of his mouth. The light turns green, but, still, he watches me.

"No, some parts are rather wonderful."

My heart beats like a thousand beating drums. I'm hyperaware of my every movement, every fluttering breath, every shake of my hand as I realize: *This is really happening.*

He finally takes his foot off the brake and we're driving again, following the traffic deeper into downtown.

"It's alright, Tori," Nate assures. "I'm glad you know."

With that reassurance, any worries I had about ruining the date with my big mouth are quelled. He's not angry at me. That's all that matters.

Soon enough, we enter the French Quarter, weaving through narrow one-way, brick-paved streets, dodging tipsy tourists and horse drawn carriages. The close buildings, fading paint, gas

70

lamps, and wrought iron balconies give a sense of old world intimacy that I've never experienced anywhere else in the United States. The New Orleans French Quarter is its own magical place unlike any other.

We cross Bourbon Street, a bright neon exclamation point amidst the quiet charm of the rest of the Quarter. Soon enough, we're past the crowd of drunk tourists and bawdy revelers searching for excess and debauchery, and we've moved onto a dark quiet street with cracked sidewalks and overhanging balconies.

Nate pulls to the curb and parks. A valet opens my door and assists me out of the car. I take a moment to get my bearings. We're in the heart of the Quarter. Jazz music plays lightly from the open window of an apartment overhead. A couple in evening finery pass us as they walk along the cracked slate sidewalk to enter the door ahead of us.

A white wooden sign spans the length of the building, with green three-dimensional block typeset declaring it to be Antoine's Restaurant. I've heard of this place—who in New Orleans hasn't? —it's the oldest French-Creole restaurant in town, known for its decadent menu and upscale elegance.

Already, I feel like I don't belong.

Nate's warm hand falls to the small of my back as he guides me inside. The shivered rush of arousal distracts me from my thoughts as we enter.

The next few moments are a blur as we're greeted by the maitre d' who quickly and discreetly escorts us past the main dining room and famous Hermes Bar. As we pass the open doors, I get a quick flash of bright white linens, shining crystal glassware, and polished café chairs, a blend of extreme new world elegance and old world French charm. The clientele is a mix of New Orleans' and visiting elite, and with a sobering burst of clarity, I again have the invading thought, *What am I doing here?*

We follow the maitre d' through the snaking hallways and intersecting courtyards. I pause at the door boldly labeled *The Dungeon,* followed by the quote:

The joys of the
table belong
equally to all
ages, conditions,
and times: they
mix with all
other pleasures
and remain the
last to console
us for their loss.
BRILLAT-SAVARIN

"I thought about requesting this room," Nate whispers darkly in my ear, his fingertips caressing down my arm, sending thrilling shivers up my spine.

"Why didn't you?" The question leaves my lips before it had a chance to fully form in my mind.

He catches my hand in his. "I don't want to scare you off too soon," he murmurs, eyes hot and intense as he raises my hand to his lips and kisses my fluttering pulse point, "And I was hoping for someplace a little more... intimate."

Arousal floods through me, deep and dark, setting my nerves on fire and keeping my limbs from working properly. My heart thunders in my ears as Nate leads me by my hand to our private dining room.

I let myself enjoy a moment of fantasy where I'm this sophisticated, gorgeous, interesting woman for whom this is a normal occurrence rather than me, Tori, a mousy diner waitress with a history of making epically bad decisions and is on the cusp of making another one.

Nate pulls me into our private dining room. A sign by the door lets us know that it's called the Tabasco Room and once I'm inside, I see why. The walls are painted a deep chili red, the same color of the peppers used for the room's namesake. A huge wood-framed mirror covers one wall and the other wall contains a display case housing rare bottles of whiskey.

There are white linens and polished china on the table. An ice bucket with a bottle of reserve label champagne chilling stands to the side. The Maitre D' pours our glasses once we're seated, then leaves.

The room is cozy, intimate, and very, very private. Nate has pulled out all the stops for tonight. Despite everything, I still want to know why.

I think I have a guess.

"Have you been here before?" Nate asks once we're alone. "I haven't but I've heard good things."

"I haven't," I murmur, looking at my menu. Some of these dishes cost more than what I make in a night. "Can't really afford it on my salary."

I sip my champagne. The bubbles pop and froth in a perfect dance of not too sweet, not too dry across my tongue.

I skim the appetizers—*huitres, escargot, crevettes,* and *ecrevisses.* They're all French words for things I eat, I know this, but, in the moment, I'm overwhelmed by the words and the options and the *prices.* I try moving on, but then there are *potages* and *salades* and *legumes* before a list of fancy sauces like *alciatore, champignons,* and *béarnaise.*

I finally reach the list of entrées, but by then I give up. I don't know what I want. I don't know why I'm here. I'm intimidated by the restaurant and the wine and the menu and the food and *him.*

Most of all him.

I can feel his eyes on me, probably studying my reactions, but I don't want to look up and confirm it. I'm hit by a wave of embarrassment.

God, what I must look like to him. Some stupid girl who's too much of a hick to be taken out in public.

I reach for my water glass to hopefully cool the burn of humiliation when I miscalculate the distance and nearly knock it off the table. Thankfully, Nate's reflexes are fast enough to prevent disaster. Because that's what I am. A disaster in a red dress.

"Why are you going through so much trouble?" I get up the nerve to ask. "We both know you're trying to get into my pants."

I stare down at the plate in front of me, afraid to see his reaction, but then curiosity gets the best of me and I glance up. He looks surprised, but not angry. Rather, he looks... impressed.

"You don't hold back, do you?" he comments with a chuckle. "I like that."

After years of Brady bullying me after I speak my mind, it's absolutely shocking to have such a different reaction.

That freedom from fear energizes me, makes me feel daring.

"Well?" I challenge him to say different.

"You're absolutely right," he confirms, "I do want to 'get in your pants'. I won't deny it when it's absolutely true that I often think about fucking you."

That hits me like a ton of bricks. I'm both offended and so fucking incredibly turned on. My nipples bead tight, catching along the lace of my bra. I'm wet, I can tell as I shift in my chair. How did I end up in this man's fantasies?

I gape at him like a fish, mouth opening and closing, trying to get a question out—What? Why? How?

He catches my hand in his and guides my arm across the table, slowly rotating my hand until it rests palm-up on the white table cloth. My wrist looks so small in his grasp.

A shiver runs through me as he caresses the inside of my wrist, tracing along the sensitive skin of my forearm, the sensual scratch of calloused fingertips along the veins make my hair stand on end. All my focus is on the dragging scrape of his fingers.

Then he whispers, voice husky with desire, "I think about tasting your sweet pussy as you lie tied to my bed... you on your knees blindfolded and the wet drag of your hot mouth on my cock… the way you're going to writhe and moan as I fuck you until you come so hard you see stars…"

He pulls my hand to him, kisses my palm, and as he looks at me through his lashes, he murmurs, "I hope by the end of the night, you'll be fantasizing the same thing."

ELEVEN

Tori

His salacious proposal echoes in my ears, bouncing through my head, leaving me stunned silent, too shocked and turned on to respond. It's so easy to imagine doing what he says, just letting go and submitting to any hedonistic fantasy he suggests. And, the way it sounds, he's barely warmed up.

But as much as I want to throw myself at him, I also know what it's like to dive head first into a fantasy only to be bitten by the reality that the pretty fantasy is nothing more than camouflage for the pit viper hiding beneath the surface.

People say when something sounds too good to be true, it usually is.

"So you don't actually want to date me. You just want to sleep with me," I reply, keeping my face neutral. The way his eyebrow shoots up, my reaction surprised him. "You're putting a lot of effort into it. Why?"

He opens his mouth to respond, but I interrupt. Maybe I'm still wound up from what happened in the car, maybe I'm just intimidated and out of my element because of this restaurant, but, whatever the reason is, I have to stop him. This feels like a matter of self-preservation. If I let him talk his way out of this, I'm going to capitulate and fall into the fantasy. And that's where the snakes are, I'm sure of it.

"Don't deny it," I continue, my heart beating out of my chest with anxious, fluttering, staccato nerves. I can't believe I'm saying this out loud. "Private room, reserve label champagne, a menu of food I can't pronounce. This is going to be a crazy expensive dinner. It feels like you're paying me for sex using this meal as currency."

I can tell he doesn't appreciate that one bit, but I keep going, "I don't know what other kinds of women you've been with, but I'm not that easy. I can't be bought. Least of all with a meal."

By the end of my declaration, Nate's eyebrow is near his hairline. Yeah, he definitely wasn't expecting this reaction from me. Frankly, I wasn't expecting it from myself, and there's a little vixen that I hide deep inside me that is wailing "Noooo" while pulling her hair and stomping her feet. The part of me that hasn't been laid in a year kind of agrees with her.

Nate leans back in his chair and takes a sip of his drink, deliberating on how to respond.

Suddenly, all the nerves and flutters and panic are gone. I've got this. I'm standing up for myself. I'm not going to allow myself to be used like some sex toy. I am advocating for myself and my needs.

"You know," he drawls, expression inscrutable, "some women drop their panties simply because I'm Nathanial Stone."

"And let me guess," I smirk with a lift of my own eyebrow, "if your name doesn't work, a ride in your fancy car and an expensive dinner does the trick?"

"Maybe," he concedes.

"Nate," I croon. "Even you said it. I'm not like other women."

"No," he grins. "No, you most certainly are not."

It feels like a line, and I go cold. Even though it was done as banter, I was serious about everything I said.

I've done this before with Brady. I let myself get pulled in by the smooth lines and the nice cars and fancy dinners, and look where it got me. And Brady is in the amateur league compared to Nate.

I can't lose myself again.

"I'm sure you say that to all the girls," I reply, pushing my chair back from the table. "Nathanial. Nate. Thank you for this but I can't stay."

Now, really for the first time, he looks shocked, absolutely baffled by the change in the evening.

"Listen, Nate," I say as I stand up, "I'm sure you're not a bad guy. I even admire how direct you're being about what you want. I just don't think I'm what you're looking for."

As I walk away from the dining room, everything in me is screaming at me to turn around.

I keep walking.

TWELVE

Nate

Well, fuck.
That did not go how I expected.
This is going to be harder than I thought.

THIRTEEN

Tori

I can't believe I just walked away like that. Oh my god.

I'm standing on the sidewalk in front of the restaurant, trying to figure out how I'm going to get home. Guess I didn't think that part through before walking out without a ride.

I am woman, I tell myself as I dig into my purse for my phone to call Elizabeth to see if she can come pick me up, *I can... shit*.

My phone isn't in my purse. It's still on the charger at home. Now what?

There's a group of drunk frat boys staggering towards me, and I try to step out of their path, still digging through my purse and hoping that my phone will magically appear.

Suddenly, one of the dudebro/frat-guys stumbles into me, his breath stinking like the rancid beer in the street gutters, before his hazy gaze latches onto my boobs.

"You're hot," dudebro slurs. "Wanta show me your tits?"

He stretches a shaky hand out to grab at my boob. I dodge, shifting away, and his other hand goes for my butt. I zag away, swatting at his searching hands with my purse. He loses his balance on the uneven sidewalk and falls back into the street, landing on his ass in a murky beer-puddle.

"Didn't your mother teach you not to treat women like that?" I ask, glaring down at him.

"It's time for your friend to go sleep it off," Nate orders from behind me. "Take him back to your hotel. Now."

The strength and dominance in his tone make me shiver.

It also works on the pack of dudebros, who grab their friend and run off, giving a few last glances at the famous celebrity standing beside me.

"Are you alright?" he asks, looking me over with concern.

"Yeah, I used my trusty purse to fend off his wandering hands," I try to joke, gesturing at Elizabeth's loaner handbag.

The fact is, though, I'm kind of shaken up.

It's like Nate *senses* it, because suddenly he's pulling me into his arms, hugging me close, cradling my head against his broad chest as I breathe the warm coffee-sandalwood-musk of *him* deep into my lungs. I just float in the moment, basking in the scent of him, the reassuring press of his arms around me, the sound of his heart beating in his chest, my breath matching his in-and-out, in-and-out...

I don't know how long we stand there, hugging each other tight in the middle of the sidewalk outside of one of the most famous restaurants in New Orleans, but we do, until I come back to myself, realizing that I'm clutching Nate like a clingy octopus when the whole reason I got into this situation was that I decided that I didn't want him.

Liar, that voice in the back of my head accuses, and it's that which makes me let go of him and step away.

God, the way I threw myself into his arms is humiliating, *especially* after running out on him in the restaurant.

But Nate acts like our hug didn't happen, or at least didn't mean anything, inquiring, "Do you have a ride home? Do you want me to stay with you while you wait for them?"

I think that hug made my brain fuzzy because I can't figure out what he's talking about. *Ride? Oh, yeah, I was trying to call Elizabeth…*

"Not that I don't think you're fully capable of fending off drunk frat boys who can't hold their liquor," he continues, joking, "I saw how well you wielded your mighty purse."

"Just call me a modern day Joan of Arc," I quip, desperate to be just as nonchalant as him. But I have to wonder, "Why didn't you jump in to stop them? That seems right up your alley."

"Did you want me to?" he counters.

I take a moment to really think about it. "I don't need to be saved."

"I saw that. You wield your weapon well. I regret that you had to, though. The mob inside kept me from arriving sooner to lend a helping hand," he nods back at the restaurant.

The lobby is packed, a detail I don't think I noticed when I was escaping. A couple of curious people peer out the window at us.

"Though you, apparently, didn't need one after all. You appeared well in control of the situation, which, frankly, the more I learn about you, the less that surprises me. You're quite a woman, Tori."

His compliment warms me from the inside, even though I don't want it to. It also makes me see him in a different light. Maybe he really does see me for me.

"So, your ride? Are they coming?" he presses.

Oh, yeah. That.

"I seem to have left my phone at home…" I wince.

"Do you like hamburgers?" he asks. "Because I don't know about you, but I'm still hungry. And I know a place if you don't mind the wait. I promise I have no ulterior motives. It's just a burger."

That's how I find myself getting drunk on a street corner twenty minutes later.

Nate takes us to some hole-in-the-wall on the edge of the Quarter. It's a small, inconspicuous green clapboard building on the corner of Esplanade Avenue and Dauphine Street, and the only way you'd even know it was there is by the tiny wooden sign over the door naming it *Port of Call* and the huge crowd of people waiting outside.

When we first arrive, Nate pushes our way inside to put our name on the wait list before fighting through the wall-to-wall crowd of people to make a hole for us at the bar.

The man, Mr. Sexiest Man Alive, himself, actually put his name on a wait list like everyone else here. He didn't try to use his name or his money to get seated faster or get the best table, which is exactly what Brady would do if he ever deigned to step into a place like this. That detail impresses me the most out of everything I've learned about Nate Stone.

While we wait for a bartender to notice us, I finally get a moment to look around and take in the place. It's dark inside, like *really* dark, and most of the light comes from the neon Budweiser and Miller Light signs above the bar. Old-school rope fishing nets hang above our heads and drape down to the half-wall that separates the bar area from the nine-table seating area, and I realize it's supposed to be some kind of *pirate bar*. It's fantastic.

"There's seating in the back, too," Nate yells over the noise. "Don't worry, it's worth the wait."

Just then, the bartender delivers a giant, juicy hamburger and an overloaded baked potato to the guy sitting on the stool next to me. My stomach growls.

"I totally believe you," I say, eyeing the other guy's burger hungrily.

Nate laughs before finally catching a bartender's attention. I watch the bartender's face. If he recognizes Nate, he sure isn't showing it.

Nate orders a beer for himself and a Monsoon for me.

"What is it?" I ask, taking the 32oz white plastic cup with the restaurant's name emblazoned across it.

"Fruit juice and rum," Nate replies, paying for our drinks before leading us outside and away from the press of the crowd.

"You don't want one?" I ask, taking a sip. Oh my god, it's fruity and rummy and so good.

"Not if I'm driving," he laughs.

He's got a point. Three sips in and I can already feel it. This thing is dangerous.

He has us standing in the shadow of the house next door, out of the way of the milling crowd. Most of the people are clutching big white cups like mine. I totally get it because this thing is awesome.

But it occurs to me, "Aren't you worried that someone will recognize you?"

"Not really. It's late, it's dark, people are drunk. So far, when I come here, luck's been on my side. It's not like they're expecting to find *Nathanial Stone* waiting outside a dive on a Friday night. But if you're worried, here," he reaches up and ruffles his hair, the perfect strands standing up in every direction. He shoots me a mischievous grin that makes him look like a sexy, unrepentant schoolboy. "Camouflage."

He's right. No one appears to pay any attention to us as we wait on the sidewalk for our names to be called. As I listen to Nate chat amicably about his favorite New Orleans dives and how everything's changed since Hurricane Katrina, I tell myself to slow down on the Monsoon because, holy shit, this thing is strong. But it's one of those things where you don't even notice you're sipping it until you've reached the bottom of the cup and the hidden cherries and orange slices beneath the ice. *Score. Cherries.*

I dig one out of the cup, popping it in my mouth, closing my eyes and savoring the delicious burst of sugary sweet delight. I suddenly realize that Nate has gone silent, his words stopped mid-sentence to stare at me as I eat my delectable fruit. His eyes are

84

dark, hooded as he watches me, and suddenly my mouth is dry and I don't know what to think.

"Cherry?" I say, offering him the second one between the pinch of my fingers.

His eyes never leave mine as he slowly, ever so slowly, leans forward and plucks the red fruit from between my finger tips, his soft lips grazing my skin, sending electrical waves through all my nerve endings. Wow.

"Yum," he says hoarsely.

Now I'm the one who's at a loss for words and we descend into lust-filled silence until Nate's name is called moments later.

Soon enough, we're following the hostess to a dark table in the corner. The menu is limited: salads, burgers, and steaks, all with baked potatoes. I'm starving. After that drink, and the wow moment between Nate and I, I'm ready to eat the whole cow.

Our server comes for our order. By the way her eyes widen and her jaw drops the tiniest bit, she probably recognizes Nate, but she keeps it professional and doesn't say anything. Just by how good these drinks are, I bet he's not the first celebrity to step through those doors.

We both order cheeseburgers and loaded baked potatoes, and, screw it, I want extra pickles on the burger and extra cheese on both the burger and potato, and, hell, extra sour cream on the potato, too. And extra bacon. Because, bacon. And, while we're at it, another Monsoon because these things are awesome.

Nate grins at me like I'm hilarious, because I am, damn it, and moves to iced tea for himself and whispers to the server waitress woman about also getting me a water.

Not that I have to drink the water because I don't. My decision.

"I like that you're you," he says once the server waitress woman leaves. "You're honest and direct and not afraid to be yourself."

"That's me," I exclaim with an exaggerated shrug of my shoulders. "Kind of hard to be anything but myself."

I *might* be drunk. Maybe. Possibly. Can't really tell. This drink is *awesome.*

"I love this place," I declare, looking around at everyone. "It's so much better than the other, fancy shmancy place. *These are my people.*" I gesture at the room.

He laughs. "Yeah. I should have taken you here first."

"Nope," I point to him. "You would have gotten me drunk and tried to do dirty, dirty things to me. I, sir, am not that kind of girl. I cannot be wooed with booze and food."

"No, no you can't. I've learned my lesson," he contends, "but I like that about you."

"What? That I'm a prude who can't hold her booze?" I ask, taking a big sip from the new Monsoon that magically appears next to me.

"No," he disagrees, "that you speak up when you're uncomfortable. You don't let me walk over you."

"Nope, no I do not, Mr. Movie Star." I nod before sticking a fork in the drink to fish out a cherry. Because cherries are awesome, too.

Our cheeseburgers and potatoes arrive. My burger is piled high with delicious cheddar cheese and the potato is drowning in cheese and sour cream. This is what heaven on a plate looks like.

"You know your boundaries and you stick to them. Most women, most *people*," he amends, "don't do that. They just crumble with a little pressure. But you don't, and I think that's an admirable trait."

"Well I don't know about that," I respond, taking my first bite. "Holy crap, so *good*…"

I moan out loud because *oh my god, this is the best*, and Nate's eyes go dark again. Yeah, I would totally do him if I wasn't a prude and, like, holding onto my sense of righteous morality.

I get back on track, "I have this ex, Brady, and you want to talk about doormats? That was me. And I decided one day that, nope, I'm not going to be a doormat anymore. I've spent enough time being bulldozed over and ruining *my* life for some guy and I'm just not going to do it anymore. But Nate?" I lean in close. "It was really nice that you wanted to take me to a nice restaurant, even though this one is better. It means a lot to me. Especially since 'nice' to Brady means the two-for-one pizza and beer combo at the bowling alley."

"So why did you stay with him?" Nate asks nonchalantly, taking a bite of his burger.

"Because I'm stupid? Because I thought I was in love?" I shrug. "And probably because I gave up everything I worked so hard for to be with him and I was like: In for a penny, in for a pound... Like I said, stupid."

"Or loyal," he suggests.

"Just call me Fido," I respond. "It didn't matter how hard he kicked me, I'd keep running back."

It gets quiet on Nate's side of the table and I look up from my potato to see him glaring daggers at the wall. I go over what I just said... Oops.

"Figuratively kicking," I rush to clarify. "I was talking in metaphors. There was no actual kicking. Brady did a lot of awful things, but he never hit me. Promise."

Nate studies my face and, despite the alcohol probably muddying my expression, realizes that I'm telling the truth.

"Good," he says softly. "No one deserves to go through that."

That makes me smile. Beneath the Hollywood swagger and charm, Nathanial Stone is really kind of sweet.

And hot. Like, burn my panties off hot.

I take a big gulp of water because I need to get a hold of myself.

Fortify, Tori. Fortify.

"I'm probably telling you way more than I should on a first date." Wait. I backtrack. "Not that this is a date anymore. It's dinner. Between friends. Acquaintances, really. People. Humans. Hamburgers between humans."

Crap. He's staring at me with what I'm starting to think is his thinking-about-me-naked-stare. And I'm pretty sure I'm too drunk to resist whatever's going to come out of his mouth next.

"Is that still what this is, Tori?" he asks, voice deep like chocolate-covered sex, his hooded slate blue eyes becoming the center of my world in that moment. "Hamburgers between humans?"

"Maybe?" I answer, not sure anymore, thoughts hazy from Nate and the drink.

"Is that all you want this to be? Dinner between people?"

"I don't know," I whisper, unsure of what's up or down, only that I have to answer him. I have to tell the truth. "No."

"Tell me, Tori," Nate beckons, "could Brady make you come?"

FOURTEEN

Tori

Dear god, I think I'm dying.

My head pounds with the cadence of a thousand tap dancers on steel drums. The light slipping in through the open blinds burns my retinas through my closed eyelids. And if I move, there's the strong possibility that I'm going to barf everywhere.

So this is what people say when they talk about bad hangovers. Even my toenails hurt.

Someone—Elizabeth? —left a glass of water and a couple pain relievers on my nightstand. What a life saver.

A few minutes after the water and meds, I start to feel like my head isn't a black hole collapsing in on itself and I can think.

My memory of last night gets fuzzy around the time the hamburgers arrived at the table, so I lie back in bed and try to remember what went on the rest of the night.

How did I even get home? Why am I only in my underwear and why is my dress in a ball on the floor? Did I..? Did we..?

My phone dings on the bedside table—apparently I left my phone on the charger rather than taking it with me last night—and pain shoots through my temple until I see the name on my phone.

Nate.

I dive for the phone, nearly knocking it and my water glass off the table as I scramble to read what he said.

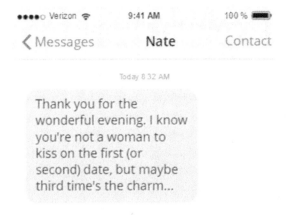

Thank you for the wonderful evening. I know you're not a woman to kiss on the first (or second) date, but maybe third time's the charm...

I guess that means we didn't sleep together; the discovery brings along with it a confusing muddling of relief and disappointment.

What did happen, though?

I think hard, attempting to remember what happened last night. I remember the car ride... Storming out of Antoine's... Then fruity drinks that pack a punch and the dimly lit interior of Port of Call...

Tell me, Tori... Could Brady make you come?

Oh, yeah. I definitely remember that moment. How Nate's voice got all deep and sexy despite how loud the bar was. How the sensual look in his eye as he asked his question got me so hot I thought I'd explode right then. How, between the booze and the bar and the inappropriate question that somehow turned me on faster than has ever happened before, I became a blushing, bashful, tongue-tied idiot.

Even alone in my room, I'm blushing. And, oh god… I think I answered the question. I duck under my bedcovers, mortified. I can't believe I answered the question!

I scramble trying to remember what exactly I said.

I remember suddenly feeling shy. Blushing. Getting incredibly over-heated and drinking a big gulp from the Monsoon. I couldn't make eye contact with Nate, who had me pinned with his hot gaze. And I really couldn't stop blushing, especially when that quirking, sexy eyebrow went up as he waited for me to answer.

As the memory comes back to me more clearly, I realize that I didn't *actually* verbally answer. I shrugged. Like, *I don't know.*

Nate asked the meaning behind the shrug with a "Is that a 'No' or an 'I don't know'?"

I kept drinking my drink, not looking up because I knew that I'd have to meet his piercing gaze. So I shrugged again.

"If you don't know, then the answer is probably 'No'," he declared.

"He was my first boyfriend," I said around the straw. No wonder I'm so hung over.

"Has anyone?" The rest of the question was strongly implied. Even pretty damned drunk by that point, I knew what he was asking.

"There is nobody else."

Nate sucked in a deep breath, eyes flaring with desire.

"One day, pretty Tori," he murmured, "you're going to let me in."

He took a moment to sip his drink, letting that sink in before continuing. "I'm not going to deny that I want to fuck you. I can't promise a future or that I'll be some sniveling boyfriend who pines away after you once I go back to L.A. But I will say that I have plans for you if you say yes.

"I *can* promise you that I'm going to take you to new heights that you've never imagined. That I'll make you feel pleasure so intense that you forget your name. I'll fuck you so good, for so long that the only thing you'll crave is my hands on your skin, my cock deep in your pussy.

"If you let me, Tori, I'll open up a whole new world to you. I'll make you fly."

FIFTEEN

Tori

There's a knock on the door and Elizabeth pops her head inside.

"Good, you're awake," she grins. "Tell me everything."

She bounds across the room and throws herself on my bed. Oh god.

"Oops," she winces, contrite. "Seems like you had a really good night."

The conversation plays over in my head and I start blushing all over again.

"Oh my god!" she exclaims. "Did you sleep with him?"

I jump to insist that "No! No. I didn't. We didn't. Nothing happened. It was just... no. Nothing happened."

Finally, the rest of the night comes to me. I pretty much slept the whole ride back to Boden. It wasn't until Nate parked the car in front of Elizabeth's house that I woke up. And, shit, I think I was drooling. Crap.

I remember how I was thinking that if he pressed, I would have let him inside to have his dirty way with me.

Oh no, I think I told him that, too. I blush at the memory.

But I also remember how he didn't say anything as he helped me out of the car. He led me to the front door and unlocked it for me when my hand was too shaky to get the key in the lock.

Nate was the one who helped me in the house and brought me a glass of water and tucked me into bed.

Sometime in the night I must have gotten hot and thrown off my dress. That would explain waking up in just my bra and underwear.

Nate was a perfect gentleman. He didn't push or pressure me. He didn't take advantage. I mean, I know that should be the default reaction, but in my experience, Brady would have taken my drunken lack of impulse control as an open invitation, which is just one more thing that makes Nate infinitely better than Brady.

I realize that I haven't said anything in awhile, and, taking a look at Elizabeth, my silence probably just cemented in her head that we did.

"We really didn't," I maintain.

"Sure," she replies, completely not buying it.

"He wants to, though," I say, glancing away, unable to look her in the eyes. "For some reason, he really seems to want me."

"And why wouldn't he? You're awesome," she replies with complete conviction.

"You know me. Guys don't want me. Besides Brady," I amend. "And he's pretty close to crazy, so he doesn't count. But other men don't want me. They don't flirt with me or ask me out."

"First," Elizabeth interrupts, "yes they do. You just don't realize it."

"Uh, I think I would notice being asked out," I respond.

"No, you don't, I promise. Business has picked up by thirty percent since you started working at the diner, and I can promise that it's not because you make a mean piece of pie or deliver it in a timely manner with a smile. Guys trip over themselves to get a seat in your section. There is definitely flirting, and I've more than once overheard one of them suggest meeting up with you after work, but you seem to never catch it."

I know I'm looking at her like she's crazy. "Are you sure you're not hallucinating this?"

"Positive," she grins. "No offense, but you're kind of oblivious when it comes to men. So I'm not shocked that it takes someone spelling it out for you for you to catch it."

I sit back on the bed and think about what she said. Huh. It does explain some of the weirder encounters I've had over the years.

"But it doesn't really explain why *Nathanial Stone* of all people is flirting."

"Does it matter?" she asks. "He's hot. He wants you. You're single. You're amazing. There is no reason to say no unless you don't want him back. Which we both know is a bald faced lie."

All very true.

"And if he's anything like his brother?" She winks. "He's going to show you a fucking fantastic time. Yowza."

My head is going in a thousand directions, not helped at all by the lingering hangover.

"Do you want my advice?" she asks.

"Sure, since you're going to give it to me anyway," I reply with a tired smile.

"You know me so well," she grins, then becomes serious. "Tori, stop worrying about it. If you want to pursue this, do it. If you don't, then don't. But I think you should. Don't worry about the future, have fun. It's OK to be with Mr. Right Now, even if he's not Mr. Right."

She lets that sink in for a moment, then poses the question, "When you're 80, looking back on your life, and we're old women sitting in rockers on the front porch, ask yourself if you'll have regretted not giving this a shot? Think about it. You don't have to know right now."

The thing is, I think I do know the answer.

"Next question," she continues. "You never answered me. How was the date?"

"Besides getting drunk?"

"Yeah, besides that."

I'm honest when I say, "It was kind of perfect."

SIXTEEN

Tori

Elizabeth is sweet enough to make me drunk brunch—a bacon-egg-avocado sandwich on Texas toast and a red Gatorade—before she leaves for the diner, so my hangover is at a dull queasy throb by the time I arrive at the Finewhile for my afternoon shift.

I'll deny it to the day I die, but when I step inside the diner, my eyes go straight to "Nate's booth" in the corner, and when I see that the occupants are two guys from the refinery, I'm more disappointed than I probably should be. I tell myself I'm being silly as I walk to the back to put away my bag and clock in. I'm acting like a middle schooler with her first crush. I'm a grown ass adult. I should act like it. None of this ridiculous pining and heart-fluttering nonsense.

Really, I made a fool out of myself last night and probably scared him off, anyway. He was just being nice with the text he sent this morning. It didn't mean anything.

I tell myself that again as I step onto the floor and begin my shift. I guess it doesn't work since I look at the door every time someone comes inside. At one point, I nearly threw a sweet tea off my tray into a man's lap because I whipped around so fast to check the door. The young mom and her toddler were most definitely *not* Nathanial Stone.

Yep. I blew it.

Not that I *really* wanted anything to do with him, I try to tell myself. The disappointment I'm feeling is only about losing a potential friend. That's it.

Liar.

Yeah, well. Whatever gets me through the day.

I spend the rest of the day talking myself down, and by the time five o'clock rolls around and Nate hasn't come to take his usual place in "his" booth, I'm completely convinced that my ridiculous drunken behavior last night ruined everything.

Not that there was an "everything" to ruin, but what there was, I ruined it.

A few minutes later, I go to make a new pot of coffee and find that whoever had the breakfast shift forgot to restock the coffee grounds. It's annoying and if it becomes a regular habit, I'm going to have to talk to Elizabeth about it, but in the meantime, I have to stop taking care of my tables to do their job.

After a quick check to make sure my tables can deal with me being gone for a few minutes, I run to the pantry to grab more from the backup supply. While I'm in there, I hear the bell ding again. My heart jumps like it has all day, and, like I have all day, I try to push aside the feeling with another self-lecture about how I'm being a ridiculous middle school girl who can't keep her hormones in check.

The lectures obviously aren't working, so as I grab a couple other things that are getting low out front, I work on reasoning with myself. The guy is busy trying to put a multi-million dollar movie into production. He has an office he can work out of that has *a lot* less distractions than the diner (and probably better WiFi, too). He probably has super important people he has to visit to discuss super important movie stuff. So his absence from the diner might not be personal at all and I'm just being ridiculous.

Ridiculous does seem to be the word of the day today.

I turn to leave the pantry only to realize I'm not alone. The box of powdered sugar falls from my hands, landing on the ground in an impressive puff of wintery white.

It's Nate. He's gorgeous, as always, with his casual heather grey t-shirt pulling tight across his broad shoulders as he strides across the few feet between us.

"I'm going to kiss you now unless you stop me," he says. The next thing I know, his strong hands are on my cheeks and his hot mouth is on mine.

The kiss is different than I expected. It's slow and tender, his lips soft and warm against mine. He tastes sweet, like the powdered sugar I spilt and the coffee with chicory he's always drinking. It's a perfect first kiss.

My eyes flutter closed and I sink into him, the tiny hairs on my body standing up as his hand combs through my hair, the pull and tug turning me on so fast I gasp. He uses that as an invitation to deepen the kiss, tilting my head and dipping his tongue to lick and taste and dart against mine.

My knees go weak and I sag into him, pressing against the hard planes of his strong body, feeling the rigid push of *him* against my hip. *At least I'm not the only one affected*, floats through my mind, as I catch his lip between mine and suck.

That must do something for him because he suddenly groans and one of his hands leaves my hair to skim down my back where it reaches my ass to push me closer to him. And, oh my god, I'm close enough to feel every thick, hard inch of him.

I bask in the feeling of the most incredible man pressed against me. I can barely think, but what does filter through the raging swirl of heat and hot and hormones is the thought that I never imagined that a kiss could be so good.

This is the best kiss of my life. Of any life. I wish it would never stop.

But, alas, soon enough, Nate pulls away, his humid breath panting hotly against my cheek. I'm really not lying, I can barely feel my feet and so I lean against him, trying futilely to regain my breath. Talk about *take my breath away*.

"I wanted to do that last night—since I first saw you, really—but I wanted you to remember it," he murmurs, voice still hoarse from our amazing kiss. "I'm so glad I did."

He leans down and gives me a small, teasing peck, just enough for a dipping taste of his tongue that leaves me weak and breathless again.

"How are you feeling?" he asks, voice laced with concern.

"I can't feel my knees," I respond, mind reeling, as I slump against his muscled chest, nuzzling the soft material of his shirt.

His silent chuckles puff against my hair, and that sends a shiver of warmth down my spine. I didn't know kissing could be that mind blowing. What's the *sex* going to be like?

He laughs out loud and with a blush of embarrassment, I realize I said that out loud.

"Oh god," I mumble, trying to burrow further into his chest.

He rubs a soothing hand along my back, hugging me closer, and I breathe in his amazing scent. I could just lose myself in this man.

Far off, I hear the tinkle of a bell and Nate backs away. There's a powdered sugar handprint on his shirt. Oops.

A whimper escapes from the back of my throat as he strokes up my arm to cup my face in his hand.

"Soon enough, beautiful," he promises, "but, for now, you have a diner full of customers who probably are wondering where their waitress has gone off to."

Oh yeah. I forgot I was at work.

"Right," I respond, cheeks flushing as I take a step back on wobbly knees. "Work. Gotta pay those bills."

I pat my hair, hoping to push back any stray hairs that might have been pulled from my ponytail. "How do I look? Can I go into public like this?"

Nate scans me, eyes hot and thorough, taking in every detail. "You look delicious, like a beignet, covered in sugar."

His mouth captures mine again, tongue taking advantage of my surprised gasp as I go back to clinging on to him. But just as quickly he steps back, leaving me breathless and shockingly aroused.

I hear Pat the fry cook call out that an order's up, and I guess I really do have to leave our little cocoon and get back to work.

"I'm going to take you out again," Nate says to my departing back.

"And I might just let you," I reply, turning to throw him a wink over my shoulder as I step out into the dining room.

Because I'm looking behind me, I don't have any warning when I hear, "Hey, sweet cheeks, got some sugar for me?"

The shock on Brady's face when Nate steps out of the kitchen with me is sweet, particularly after that absurd pick up line he tried to give me.

The way Brady's face quickly darkens with rage is not so sweet.

I watch, frozen, as Brady's eyes sweep back to me and scan me, looking for evidence as to what just went down between me and Nate in the pantry. I can almost feel the way his gaze locks on my loosened pony tail, the black apron that's gray with powdered sugar, the crumpled tail of my shirt that I forgot to tuck back in, my kiss-bruised lips. Then Brady's eyes go to the white handprint on Nate's shirt.

If at all possible, he gets even angrier.

If I don't do something, this is going to get ugly fast.

SEVENTEEN

Nate

So this must be the infamous douchebag ex-boyfriend. Brian? Grady? *Brady.*

Yeah, I decide, getting a good look in, *the name fits.*

The guy is in a pair of bright Easter egg plaid shorts with a mint green polo half tucked in the front and the collar half popped in the back. He's got soccer sandals on his feet, a fist size belt buckle at his waist, and a LSU baseball cap on his head. How is this guy expecting anyone to take him seriously?

Besides, the way Tori is looking at this douchebro, there's no way he's a threat. However, it appears he hasn't gotten the memo yet if the scowl on his face is anything to go by.

Tori looks like she was ravished. Her skin glows, her eyes shine, her lips are moist and kiss swollen. My powdered sugar handprints frame her ass. She looks like I branded her.

I know the exact moment when Brady figures out what went on in the pantry. This guy wouldn't last an hour in Vegas.

That this douchebag thinks he still has a chance with her wells up aggression in me that I didn't know existed. It makes me want to smash my fist through his bro-tastic face before dragging

Tori to the closest surface and fucking her for all to see that she's mine.

She's mine.

That thought shocks me back to normal. I never get territorial or jealous about women. It just doesn't happen.

What's going on? Why am I so territorial *and* jealous over Tori that I'm ready to beat this dickweed into the ground so that he knows Tori's off limits?

I stare hard at Tori's face, trying to figure it out. What makes Tori different?

I don't get long to think about it because Brady decides to make a scene. Asshole.

"Who's the clown, Tor-Tor?" Douchebag asks.

Clown? Really? That's what he's going with? OK then. What a joke.

Tori seems to think the same thing if her massive eye roll is anything to go by.

"You know who he is," she impatiently sighs. "Give it up. What do you want?"

"I wanted to see for myself if the rumors are true," he smirks. He looks me up and down like *I'm* beneath *him*—which is a riot—before continuing, "Looks like they are."

Tori sighs heavily. I'm glad to see she's not buying into this jackass's games. "What rumor, Brady?"

"I think you know," the jackass brays smugly. My fist is starting to itch from my restraint on holding back from wiping that grin off his face. I don't think of myself as a particularly violent man, but an angel would struggle to keep calm in his presence.

I bite back a laugh when Tori hisses, "You know I don't *actually* care what people are saying, right? So either say whatever it is you came here to say or leave. Either way, you need to hurry up because I have to get back to work."

Brady's douchebag face turns an impressive shade of fuchsia before his look turns mean, and he says with a twisted grin,

"Everybody's talking about how you're whoring around with Mr. Hollywood here. How you're some gold digging slut who gives it up to whatever rich dick slides into town."

I'm halfway around the counter, fists ready to pummel this fucker, when Tori's small hand presses against my chest to stop me. I look down at her, trying to figure out why the hell she wants to stop me from shoving my foot up his ass, but she isn't looking at me.

Instead, Tori stares Brady down, a dangerous eyebrow raised as she smirks at her ex with an impressive amount of sneering disdain.

I can just tell, Tori's about to let him have it. And by the way he keeps on smirking like he just made the kill shot, dumb shit is too stupid to realize he just made a fatal error. This is going to be good.

Tori laughs in his face, which just confuses the poor sucker. "I'm guessing that by 'everyone', you mean your mother."

The poor bastard gapes at Tori like a fish and tries to bluster his way out of it, but Tori doesn't give him the chance.

"I'm pretty sure 'slut' and 'whore' are the nicest words she's used to describe me," she drops her voice low and gestures at the restaurant goers, most of whom are ignoring us. "I've always wondered... Does your mama know you call out her name in bed?"

"Fuck you, bitch," Brady growls, raising his hand to hit Tori.

I jump between them, grabbing his swinging arm, balling my other fist to slam it down his throat, when a reedy old voice orders, "You better back away now, boy, if you know what's good for you."

The voice belongs to an old diner regular. The guy is probably in his 80s and is struggling to stand from the booth he always sits at with his wife, but old age and creaky bones aren't stopping him as he scolds, "Go along now and leave Miss Tori alone. You've had your say. It's time to get out of here."

There's a chorus of agreement from the other regulars, both men and women, and a few other guys stand up to side with the old guy. Brady knows he's lost, but the shithead just has to get the last word in.

"I'd say 'Fuck you', Tori, but I already have," Brady smirks before turning and stomping out, glowering at everyone standing up against him.

"You better hope none of you work for me," he threatens as he slams the door. The bell jingles loudly in the silence of his departure.

"Did I just get everyone fired?" Tori gasps, covering her mouth in horror. Tears well in her eyes. I try to comfort her, pulling her close to my side and rubbing her back. She's so upset that I don't think she notices.

"Fuck 'em, Tori," a guy I hadn't noticed sitting in the corner calls out. "He can just try to get rid of me. There's nobody on this side of the state who can do what I do."

There's a rumble of support. At this time of the day, most of the diner patrons are retirees anyway.

"Don't worry about him none, Miss Tori," the old man proclaims. "That boy is trash, just like his momma."

"That woman always acted like she was better than the rest of us 'cause she had money from marryin' in with the Boden family, but she's always been sleazier than a dirty floor on Bourbon Street," his wife gossips. The old timers at the surrounding tables nod in agreement.

"Thank you, Gus," Tori says, squeezing the old man's hand before helping him sit back in his booth, then leaning over to hug his wife. "Nanette. You didn't have to say anything. I had it under control."

"We know, honey," Nanette coos. "We were just tired of hearing that donkey bray."

"Was ruining my digestion," Gus nods.

"I'm s—"

Gus interrupts her apology, "Don't go trying to apologize for that buffoon. You ain't got nothing to be sorry for—"

"Except maybe sorry for dating him in the first place," Nanette jokes.

Tori cracks a smile and giggles, and I know everything's going to be OK.

"Anyone up for some pie? I think this is a pie kind of day." Tori offers, "It's on house."

Without any confirmation from the diner-goers, Tori turns to the display case and starts cutting slices of apple pie. I go over to help her and I realize her hand holding the knife is shaking.

"Hey, it's OK," I murmur softly so no one can overhear. "It's over."

"I'm sorry about that," she sniffs. "I can't imagine what you must think of me now."

"I think you're amazing," I say, surprising both of us. But it's true. I do. I lean over the counter to catch her gaze and continue. "I think it says a lot about you that you had a whole restaurant full of people ready to come to your defense."

"But Brady—"

"Is a joke," I reply. "He's a mean little boy who thinks his toy was taken away. Not that you're a toy, but that's how he sees it."

"I can't believe I dated him for so long," she moans. "He's insane, right? I'm not imagining that what just happened was crazy?"

"Hey, we've all fucked some duds. I know I have," I chuckle. "There's some real crazy in my not so distant past."

"It was humiliating," Tori groans. "Now the whole town is going to know what happened."

"There's only one person who should be embarrassed, and, beautiful, it's not you," I reassure her.

She *is* beautiful in that moment, bruised but not broken, still standing tall. She's strong. She's a survivor. She's more than I ever bargained for.

"Let me take you out again."

EIGHTEEN

Tori

I'm standing on the top of a cliff staring at the water below, deciding whether I should jump or wait for the wind to push me over the edge. At this point, it's no longer a matter of if I will go over the cliff's edge, but when and how. I know that falling through the air will be a joyous, thrilling rush unlike any other I've ever experienced. What makes me hesitate to jump is the question of how the fall will end—will the water below hit me like icy bone-breaking concrete or will it accept me into its warm, loving embrace? Will I be damaged beyond all repair or will I come out of the fall better off for leaping?

The cliff, of course, is a metaphor for my life right now.

After this afternoon, after that toe curling kiss and Nate's willingness to stand up for me against Brady, my resolve to stay away from him is so weak, it's almost nonexistent. What happens next is really just a question of whether or not I jump or wait to be pushed.

As Nate drives us down a secluded, swamp-lined road, I have to wonder if the decision is going to be a little bit of both.

I also wonder where we're going because we're in the middle of nowhere with nothing of consequence for thirty miles in any direction and it's going to be dark soon.

My hungry stomach grumbles, leading me to jokingly ask, "Where are we going? And are you going to feed me first before you dump my body?"

Nate glances away from the road to give me a sexy smirk. "There are many things I want to do to your body," he promises hotly. "I can promise you that's not one of them."

Oh.

A shiver runs through me as every hair follicle stands on end from the dark lust in his voice, and suddenly I'm aware of every inch of my body, my skin. The way the soft cotton of my dress slides across the sensitive skin of my thighs. How my nipples pebble and catch against the lace of my bra. The way the most intimate part of me dampens with desire. It's like even my hair is turned on right now.

The edge of the cliff comes closer.

I take a deep breath, trying to slow my heart rate down and think through the lazy gray haze of arousal. I know what tonight is. I know that I'll soon have to decide to step, or fall, off the ledge or turn around and leave the cliff completely. A sharp stabbing pain shoots through me at the thought of walking away from Nate.

I know, *I know*, that he only promises a short affair, that my time with him will last no longer than a few brief months at best. He lives two thousand miles away and his family, besides his estranged father, have long scattered across the globe. Barring some random, unexpected event, he will have no reason to come back to Boden, to me.

Look at what happened to Elizabeth after her time with his brother. She hasn't seen Chance since. The Stone brothers are very good at leaving Boden and never looking back. And, if what happened to Elizabeth is any example, they leave a lasting, life-changing impact behind.

For Nate, I'll become some distant memory, one lover of many. For me, he'll become a highlight in my life's story, a bright spot in a sea of darkness, a burst of color in a field of beige, a time of wistful memories and "Remember when..?"

And that's if I'm lucky that fond memories are all he leaves behind. If I'm unlucky, I'll be left in a puddle of self-recriminations and despair.

I glance over at his gorgeous profile, taking in the way the setting sun sends shadows over high cheekbones and strong jaw, his plump, sensuous mouth and steel blue eyes. This is a man who leaves devastation in his wake.

And I'm a monogamous, long-term relationship, only-have-sex-when-you're-in-love kind of girl.

My anxious musings come to a swift end when Nate suddenly pulls his Tesla over and stops on an obscured gravel road that cuts through the swamp.

"We walk from here," he says, putting the car in park, stepping out into the balmy air.

"Are you sure you didn't bring us to the set for a horror movie?" I joke as he helps me out of the car.

"Pretty sure," he grins, popping open the trunk and pulling out a large picnic basket. "I can't promise that a gator won't get you, though."

"You're hilarious," I deadpan, rolling my eyes at him. I've learned in the years since moving to Boden that alligators are only a threat to small dogs and in movies.

"So where are we?" I ask as I follow him along the gravel path through the low-hanging cypress trees and deeper into the swamp.

"This is our family property. Dad used to have a hunting camp here when I was little," he explains. "He stopped taking care of it after mom died and it finally blew over during Hurricane Katrina. But the dock is still there."

Soon enough I see it ahead through the trees, an old wooden dock jutting out into the softly lapping waters of Lake Pontchartrain. Someone was here before us. There are candles and lanterns leading to a quilted blanket and mounds of pillows.

It's the most romantic thing I've ever seen.

"Nate?" I gasp, looking at him, trying to understand what's going on.

"I thought we could have dinner," he says, taking my hand as if secluded candle light picnics on a lake are a daily occurrence.

"This looks like more than dinner," I chuckle nervously, my awkward nerves on full display.

"If you agree, I hope it is," he murmurs, kissing my hand and pulling me forward.

Moments later, I'm nestled in a pile of crimson and gold silk pillows as Nate uncovers a veritable feast of tasty foods. He pours me a glass of Luca Paretti Rosé. The crisp pink sparkling wine dances across my tongue and tickles my nose as I watch him uncover a feast of tangy shrimp remoulade salad, blue crab spring rolls, and an artfully arranged platter of perfectly done beef tenderloin, chilled and surrounded by grilled vegetables, served with tangy horseradish crema.

"It all looks so good. I don't know what to try first," I whisper, looking up at him for guidance. I'm overwhelmed by the food, the ambiance, the effort, *Nate*.

"Try this," he says, pressing a cracker smeared with white-red-green deliciousness to my lips. "It's amazing."

And he's right, it's fantastic. The creamy feta and I-don't-know-what-else cheese comes together with the salty sweet of pesto and sundried tomatoes to create a whole new set of flavors that defy this plain of existence.

"Oh my god. More, please," I gasp, and Nate laughs, feeding me another amazing green cheese cracker thing.

He continues to prepare those delicious crackers for me, and himself, until we're finally out.

"I need the recipe for that," I sigh, sitting back in my pile of pillows.

"I'm sure that can be arranged," he chuckles. "For a price."

"Oh really?" I laugh. "And what would that be? My first born child? Because that thing is so good that anything less would be criminal."

He surges forward, pressing a quick, searing kiss on my lips that takes my breath away. Too soon, oh, too soon, he's pulling back, leaving me dazed and panting, wanting more.

"That's all I want," he murmurs, taking a sip from his wine glass, his gaze scorching over the rim.

I blink at him, trying to get my wits about me. "I'm sure we can negotiate."

"I'm sure we can," he chuckles, picking up his fork and stabbing a succulent shrimp in a zesty cream sauce. "Try the shrimp remoulade next."

I nod, following his instructions, and I'm not disappointed. The shrimp are tender and sweet, the remoulade sauce tangy and refreshing, and it comes together in a blend of tastes and sensations that have me going back for more.

It's somewhere in the middle of the blue crab spring rolls that I ask, "What made you want to become an actor?"

Nate's in the process of taking a bite of his spring roll, and if I had blinked, I would have missed the tiny hesitation in his chewing before he swallows and nonchalantly reaches for his wine to take a sip.

"Why does anyone move to L.A. to become an actor? Fame, money, women..."

I can't help but roll my eyes at his cavalier answer. "I'm sure those are great perks of the job. But why that career path?"

He shrugs. "It was a direction out of town. I needed somewhere to go and something to do. Acting was something that I enjoyed and was good at so that's what I chose."

I watch Nate finish the last of his spring roll before spearing a slice of the steak and swirling it in the horseradish sauce. I follow his direction, and I'm not disappointed. Perfection. The steak is tender and juicy, even chilled like it is, and the crema adds an extra *something else* that brings it to the next level. This is a meal for the ages.

As I chew, savoring every morsel, I think about what Nate just said… and what he didn't say.

I have to ask, "Why'd you leave Boden? I mean, you and your brothers all left town. You're all super successful—which is amazing—but what made y'all want to get out? So few people leave. They get jobs at the refinery or maybe someplace like the diner or the laundromat. They don't go on to become movie stars. But it's not just you. It's your brothers, too. What's different about your family?"

I don't know why I'm asking, why I'm pushing. I think I just need to understand.

Nate swirls his wine in his glass, watching the way the torchlight hits the pink liquid and the bubbles desperate to escape from within. His face isn't closed off, just contemplative, like he's thinking hard about how much he wants to share with me.

I want to tell him it's OK, he can ignore my question, we can move on like it was never asked. But if I'm going to do what he wants, be with him how he wants, I need to do it with *him*, the man he is deep inside, not just the man he shows the world.

"I just want to get to know you," I whisper. "I need to understand. Please."

I don't know why it matters so much to know him, to understand him, not if this thing between us is temporary, but it does. It matter so much.

Maybe this is some sort of test that I'm setting him up to fail in some unconscious need to protect myself. If it is, I don't mean to do it. I don't want him to fail—I want to be with him—but I don't want him to stay closed off to me. I just think that if

I'm risking so much of myself to be with him, then I need is to understand a little sliver of who he is and how he came to be this way.

As the silence stretches between us, punctuated with the soft lapping of the water, the croak of bullfrogs, and the low hums of cicadas, I realize… *I'm not going to get my answer.*

Disappointment crashes through me and steals the breath from of my lungs. It's physically painful, deep in my chest, behind my breastbone and next to my heart. I didn't realize I wanted this so badly. Not until this very moment when the possibility of what I could have with Nate is threatened.

Threatened by me.

Can I go forward as little more than strangers? Can I let myself take that risk? Will I—

"I told you how my mother died," Nate's soft voice interrupts my spiraling thoughts. "What I didn't tell you was that my father didn't stop drinking."

It takes me a moment to realize what he's doing.

He's letting me in.

At once, my fears and disappointment disappear, and the space left behind fills with the warm knowledge that he's allowing me to see past the mask of Mr. Hollywood to the man deep inside. He's allowing me to know the real Nate Stone.

Nate continues, his voice little more than a whisper, "He killed my mom with his drinking, but, for some reason—maybe because we lived in a backwoods town where he bowled with the police chief, I don't know—he didn't even get a slap on the wrist. You'd think killing his wife, the mother of his children, would be enough reason to get sober, but, no, not my dad. It just got worse. He went from just being belligerent to becoming violent."

He looks up at my sharp intake of breath only to give me a shrug like *it is what it is* before going back to his plate and taking a bite of roasted zucchini, chewing thoughtfully before saying, "I don't know how much you know about it—I'm sure Chance told Lizzie some of it, and I don't know what she told you…"

His eyes meet mine, waiting for an answer. I don't have much to say. "Not much, just that it got bad enough that Chance moved in with her family for a little bit."

My mouth feels dry so I take a sip of wine, hoping that it will help. It tastes like tears.

He gives a bitter laugh. "Chance breathing loudly was enough to send dad into a rage when dad had been drinking. It didn't matter how hard Chance tried, he was always the one dad went after first. Leo was about sixteen when mom died, and he would step in if he was there. I tried to stop it, too, but we were just kids, really, and there wasn't much he or I could do except take Chance's hits ourselves."

The thought guts me, these brave little boys stepping in front of their enraged father to protect their little brother.

The memory surfaces of Nate's steady voice behind me, warning the drunk frat boy away when we were in the French Quarter, the way his strong arms held me tight as I shook from fear afterward, and how he stepped in front of me to protect me from Brady's fist…

I realize… Nate's a protector. He has been since childhood.

Something about that sends shivers down my spine and releases a knot of tension in my belly. Whatever else may happen, he'll never intentionally try to hurt me. He doesn't have it in him.

Nate continues, "Thankfully, dad ignored Felix, for the most part. He was six when mom died, and he was already quiet and serious. He always had his head in a book, sitting silent in the corner, blending into the background. The kid's a god-damned genius, has always been, and his focus is… absolutely unbelievable to witness. Bombs could drop around him and they wouldn't rock him at all."

The pride in Nate's voice is clear. It's beautiful to see how much he loves his brothers.

115

"Leo would take us to the library to do our homework and keep us out of the house. When Leo wasn't looking, Chance and I would have Felix do our homework." He chuckles. "God, we were such shits back then. Felix would go along with it, happy to help out his big brothers and happy to be in his head where things like facts and numbers made sense. The kid's a billionaire and runs an investment management firm now, so I guess it all paid off in the end."

"And Leo?" I ask, fascinated by this poignant, bittersweet story. "The only thing I know about him is that he does something with medicine or technology, and that he's doing *very* well at it. There's always been a lot of gossip about all the four of you in the diner, but I never really paid attention to it because I never thought I'd ever have the opportunity to meet one of the famous Stone brothers." I give Nate a rueful smile.

He smiles back but his is almost wistful. "He's in biotech. His company creates inventions and technology to make the world a better place. Leo was my hero growing up, so there's a kind of poeticism to him trying to save the world now."

I smile at that, at the obvious love and respect Nate still carries for his big brother. "What's he like?"

"A lot like Felix: studious, introverted, they kept to themselves when they weren't with us. Leo's pretty brilliant too, not Felix-smart, but smarter than anyone else you'd ever come across. If he didn't go to college for football, it would've been for academics, and it'd probably still have been Harvard. He's strong, where it matters, and he did his best to protect us, above everything else."

Nate allowing me to see inside the world of his family is the most beautiful gift he could have given me, better than a thousand romantic candle-lit dinners. I treasure everything he's willing to tell me, every little nuance that went into creating the man who sits in front of me now.

"None of us were going to stand in the way of Leo getting out of Boden," he continues. "You know he tried to give up his scholarship to Harvard? He wanted to stay and take care of us, since he knew dad wasn't going to. He had this whole plan of getting a job at the refinery and saving up money to get a place for the four of us. It was Chance who finally convinced him to leave, and Leo hasn't been back to Boden since."

"Do you ever see him?" I ask.

"A fair amount, when our schedules meet up. We talk on the phone often, though."

"What about Felix?"

"I talk to him a little less than Leo, but more than Chance since he's always on the road."

"What's Felix like now? Any different?"

"Not really," he chuckles. "He's still a bit of a hermit and a massive workaholic, which I'm OK with since he's in charge of all my money. He graduated high school the same time I did. It was kind of embarrassing back then to be dumber than your twelve-year-old brother."

There's humor on his face in this moment, even though just moments ago his story was raw and painful. It's like he feels the emotions the retelling brings up, acknowledges them, and lets them go. His emotions don't define him or control him; they're merely a part of him. It's reassuring in a way I didn't know I needed.

"Where did Felix go after graduation?" I ask.

"By the time we both graduated, Leo was at MIT for grad school so we sent Felix there for undergrad so Leo could keep an eye on him. Not that Felix really needed it. He's so serious that he wouldn't know fun if it punched him... But then, Leo can be a giant tight-ass too... I'm sure they were a riot at school together."

We share a smile and he refills my glass once again before continuing, "Then there's Chance."

117

"I know he was always planning to follow the music," I interject. "At least that's what Elizabeth's said."

"You know I only knew her as Lizzie?" Nate says. "Chance's Lizzie is what I called her in my head until I finally met her."

"He talks about her?" I ask, surprised. "Still?"

"More than you would guess," he answers. "He's still hung up on her. A lot. He doesn't say anything when he's sober, but from what I've gotten from him when he's not? I don't think he's ever really moved on."

"Think something should be done about it?" I muse.

"I'm already working on it," he says with a cheeky grin.

One part of me thinks we shouldn't meddle, but then a larger part thinks something needs to change in the saga of Chance-and-Lizzie, especially if neither of them has ever gotten over the other one. If it takes a little push from fate—or Nate—then that's what needs to happen.

"You know, I'm not too surprised he has a kid he doesn't know about," Nate muses, sipping his wine.

"Why's that?" I ask, really interested to hear his perspective.

Nate shrugs, "It's not just one thing. He's always been charismatic as fuck, and between that, and, you know, some would say he's—arguably—the best looking one out of all of us—"

I scoff at that and Nate gives me a devilish grin.

"Glad to know you don't agree," he chuckles, voice turning deep and sensuous.

I blush, but I match his smoldering gaze, because, yeah, I think he's hot and I don't care if he knows it.

He grins. "Though more than one of my high school girlfriends would disagree with you."

"Then they're blind," I brazenly reply. "And stupid."

He laughs, suddenly surging forward to meet my lips with his. It's not rushed or hungry, but a joyful meeting of smiles, his on mine, in a way that makes my heart sing and my pulse flutter.

Kissing Nate feels like a new experience every time, and this time feels like the warmth of the candlelight on the dock and the buzz of champagne bubbles through my veins. It's not hurried or forced or full of fire that sputters out too soon. It's like discovering the sunrise for the first time. It's like coming home.

He slowly pulls away, eyes searching mine, searching for what, I don't know, but he must find it because there's a softness in his gaze as he sits back in his cove of pillows and pours us both the last of the wine.

As the bullfrogs and cicadas drone on and the water laps against the shore, creating its own kind of music, Nathanial Stone feeds me fresh cherries dipped in Chantilly whipped cream. The bright berries burst on my tongue, soon followed by his lips on mine, his tongue dipping in to taste the cherries for himself. This time I feel the fire and it burns me alive.

This was a night intended for intimacy and seduction. It works. I'll deal with the fallout once it happens.

I jump off the cliff.

Want to know what happens next?

Sir: The Awakening (*The Awakening Series – Book Two*) is now available on Amazon!

You can also Go Behind the Curtains on **DLHess.com** to learn more about the events, locations, and characters in *Sir* and *The Awakening Series*.

(All of my research is on my blog. I promise, you *want* to read it. You can even follow along while you're reading the books to see photos of what I'm describing and to learn why I made the choices I made.)

You should also join the mailing list for **DLHess.com** because *D.L. Hess Insiders* are the *first* to know things.

D.L. Hess Insiders will be the ONLY people to receive a copy of the first chapter of Sir3. They will get to see the cover before anyone else. If I have excerpts that don't make it into the book, D.L. HESS INSIDERS GET THEM.

Also, you can follow me on Facebook, Twitter, and Instagram @DLHessWrites!

(And, please, don't forget to review on Amazon and Goodreads!)

Many Thanks

Words cannot express my intense, overwhelming gratitude to the many people who have rallied around me to help me bring this book to life. The support I've received has been... well, it makes me teary when I think about it.

My first thanks goes to my little sister Samantha, my rock, my personal assistant, the calm at the center of the storm who catches the thousand balls that I drop.

My parents and grandmother, for always supporting me.

Jackie, who would have loved to have seen what I've accomplished. You once asked me why I didn't write romance novels. I'm sorry you never got to see it happen in person, but I can feel your hand on my shoulder now. I miss you.

Brandie, Rebecca, and Abby, my three fairy godmothers of advice and direction.

Dharti and Elijah, who came to my rescue when my previous cover designer didn't work out one week before publishing.

Ann, Darrel, Surya, and Tom, for rescuing a damsel-in-distress and creating a beautiful website.

Courtney, my grammar guru, who finds my dropped commas and missing "thats".

Sarah, who brainstorms ideas and characters with me for hours from 2000 miles away.

Kim, for the sanctuary to work in peace.

Miz Lizzie, for developing a plan so that the release of *Sir* (and my career) will be a success.

Valorie, for helping me fight to find my place in the world.

Jon, for his gentle reminders not to get lost in my head.

The Peeps, for your continued support, encouragement, and help.

Ms. Grammer, my 12th grade English teacher, who told me that one day I would write a book and that it would be great. Your comment has stayed with me since you said. I hope this one doesn't disappoint.

And Busby, my little love, the original Sir... Thanks for being the best writing partner a girl could have.

To the hundreds of family, friends, colleagues, acquaintances, and friends-of-friends who have rallied around to support me and the release of *Sir*... Thank you.

About the Author

D.L. Hess read her first romance novel when she was ten years old. It was Judith McNaught's *Once and Always*, and she spent that entire Saturday night hiding in the closet and reading until she was done. . . only to start again from the beginning.. That book left an imprint, an imprint she hopes to leave with you.

D.L. Hess grew up in Baton Rouge, Louisiana and now goes between her hometown and Los Angeles, where she works as a screenwriter. Her partner-in-crime is a nine-pound Pomeranian-Chihuahua mix named Busby Berkeley who travels with her everywhere in a carrier that looks like a purse. D.L. Hess is an avid fan of Cajun cooking, traveling, and discovering new experiences. Her travel bucket list includes cruising all the major rivers in the world. So far, she has only hit two of them.

Made in the USA
Coppell, TX
13 December 2022

89119371R00080